FREDDIE'S
SHADOW
CARDS

Jessica Brody

 PRESS

Los Angeles • New York

THIS LABEL APPLIES TO TEXT STOCK

More new books coming soon in
the School of Secrets series . . .

Next:
Ally's Mad Mystery

THE HAND
YOU'RE DEALT

The gift wasn't wrapped. The girl was surprised her father had remembered her birthday at all. There wasn't a whole lot of celebration on the Isle of the Lost, an island full of fallen villains. What did they have to celebrate? They were basically all prisoners, banished there by King Beast and his royal proclamation to rid the United States of Auradon of evil.

The girl, who was celebrating her tenth birthday that year, was used to getting dolls from her father. Not normal dolls like the ones most little girls snuggled with at night. These were voodoo dolls, full of a special kind of dark magic.

At least, they would have been, had magic been allowed on the Isle of the Lost.

But that year, on her birthday, the girl wasn't sure what to make of the object her father tossed to her during their breakfast of goblin slop and crusty bread.

It was a strange pack of cards, tied together with a piece of old yellowed string. She held the pack in her hand and studied it for a long time, turning it around and around in an effort to make sense of it.

"What are these?" she asked her father, who was humming to himself as he cut his bread. Her father liked to hum. The girl got her musical talent from him.

But as soon as she asked the question, he stopped humming and turned to her with a scowl. "I have failed you, *ma petite*, if you don't recognize a deck of Shadow Cards when you see one."

The girl's eyes widened. "Shadow Cards?" she repeated in disbelief.

Obviously, she'd heard of Shadow Cards. Her father had spoken highly of his long-lost days in the bayou when he had made a living using those dark-magic harbingers. According to her father's stories, the cards could predict a person's future. They could tell you which path to take to find what you desired most.

But she'd never seen a deck before. "*Real* Shadow Cards?"

Her father scoffed at that. "Yes, they're real."

"Do they work?" she asked.

The question seemed to anger him. He refused to meet her eye across the table.

The girl immediately knew why he was angry, and she regretted asking in the first place.

Of course they didn't work. It was the Isle of the Lost. Magic was forbidden there—which meant her father's life's work was forbidden there, too.

She untied the string that held the deck together, and fanned the cards out in her hand. A dark and creepy image stared back at her from the face of each card: a woman with three heads, a heart pierced by a sword, a castle on fire.

She grinned. "I love them. Thank you."

Her father's dark eyes darted to her. "Do you even know how to use them?"

She shook her head. "No."

That seemed to make him instantly forget his anger as he tipped his head back and released an evil cackle, like he knew a secret that she didn't. "Someday you will, *ma petite*," he said, staring intensely at her. "Someday you will."

And he was right.

SHADOW GIRL

Hi, I'm Freddie, the daughter of Dr. Facilier.

You might know my dad. He's most famous for turning princes into frogs and making deals with his "friends on the other side," among other cool stuff.

Some people call him the shadow man, but to me he's just bad old Dad.

Don't worry if you haven't heard of me yet. You soon will. I'm going to be famous one day, too. Not for shrinking heads or transforming people into frogs, like my father. That's so last generation. I'm going to be famous for singing.

I love to sing. And one day I'm going to move to the Bayou D'Orleans, where my father is from, and become a professional jazz singer. It's all I've wanted since I was a little girl.

But you can't just become a famous jazz singer. You have to

work your way up. You have to learn the ropes. Practice every day. Perform every chance you get.

And that's exactly what I'm going to do.

While most of my peeps are still stuck back on the Isle of the Lost with no Wi-Fi and no magic (major bummer), I happen to be one of the lucky few VKs (that stands for villain kids) who got to come live in Auradon.

Sounds pretty wicked, right?

It is. I mean, sort of. For the most part.

Okay, the truth is the kids here at Auradon Prep are still suspicious of me. But it's not like I care what a bunch of AKs (Auradon kids) think of me. I don't need them as friends. I have a plan. And it's pretty foolproof, if you ask me.

Because honestly, when in the history of time has a villain's plan ever gone wrong?

UNLUCKY THIRTEEN

Back when I was living on the isle, I
never would have guessed I'd be dying
to join a group of Auradon Prepsters.

What can I say? A girl's gotta sing.

Freddie couldn't believe her eyes. She stared at the sign, blinking twice to make sure her vision wasn't out of focus. But she could see just fine. And she wasn't imagining it. The sign read:

AURADONNA AUDITIONS TODAY AT 3:00!

Freddie checked the time on the clock hanging in the middle of the Auradon Prep banquet hall. It was 2:58 p.m. And the auditions were on the other side of the school, in the chapel.

Freddie started to run.

The Auradonnas were the a cappella group at Auradon Prep and they were one of the best a cappella groups in all of Auradon Kingdom. Freddie would have shrunken her own head for the chance to join the Auradonnas, but they never had spots open. So why were they suddenly holding auditions?

Did someone drop out? she wondered. *Is someone sick?*

The Auradonnas had won almost every competition in the kingdom. That was something Freddie knew only because Audrey, Princess Aurora's daughter and the lead alto of the group, never stopped blabbing about it.

Lately it seemed like the upcoming national a cappella championships were all Audrey could talk about. And how if they didn't win, she'd be forced to do something really drastic, like wear black.

Yes, Audrey had been even more stressed and cranky than usual those days.

It was mostly because some new group had just popped up that year. They were called the Sword in the Tone, and they were rumored to be out-of-this-world amazing. It was making everyone in the Auradonnas nervous.

Freddie picked up the pace, huffing and puffing as she dashed past the dorm toward the chapel. It was admittedly hard for her to run in her pin-striped red velvet dress and black-and-white ankle boots, but she did *not* want to miss this once-in-a-lifetime opportunity.

Nothing like the Auradonnas existed on the Isle of the Lost. A group of people singing in harmony without instruments? Yeah, right.

The only songs she'd ever heard when she was growing up were the dark nursery rhymes her father used to croon to her when she couldn't fall asleep. Her favorite was the one that went:

Masters of the Shadow Land,
I call upon your knowing hand.
I offer you this sinner's song
To guide the path I walk upon.

She had never known what the nursery rhyme meant, but it had always helped her fall asleep.

As Freddie darted across the tourney field, she could see the chapel in front of her. She was almost there. She just hoped they hadn't already chosen someone. Being in the Auradonnas would definitely solve *all* of Freddie's problems. Not only would it allow her to sing every single day *and* get her one step closer to her goal of becoming a famous jazz singer, but it might help with her recent boredom, too.

Ever since her best friend, CJ, Captain Hook's daughter, had set out on her great pirate adventure a few weeks earlier, Freddie had been feeling a little lonely. She didn't really have anyone to hang out and get into mischief with.

Of course, she wasn't exactly kissing frogs at the idea of hanging out with a bunch of stuffy AKs, but she supposed it was better than the alternative: sitting at the banquet hall by herself for every meal—which was basically what she did now.

When she burst through the doors of the chapel a few minutes later, the twelve girls who made up the Auradonnas were standing in a line on the stage, singing a catchy upbeat number.

Freddie instantly recognized the song. It was called "Rather Be with You." Since she'd learned that the Auradonnas existed, Freddie had memorized every part of every one of their competition songs—just in case an opportunity popped up.

Freddie had to admit the song kind of nauseated her. It was extremely bubbly and cheerful. But she didn't care. If it meant she could get into the Auradonnas and sing on that stage in two weeks for the national competition, she'd sing "Bibbidi-Bobbidi-Boo" if she had to.

Freddie ran down the center aisle of the chapel. As soon as she reached the stage, the group stopped singing.

Freddie bent over, resting her hands on her knees, as she struggled to catch her breath. "Sorry." *Gasp.* "I'm." *Pant.* "Late." *Wheeze.*

Audrey stepped forward from the line, putting her hands on her hips. "Um, what are you doing here?" she asked in her typical snooty voice. "We're trying to rehearse."

Freddie stopped panting and glanced at each of the twelve singers in turn. She was waiting to find *someone* who looked like she knew why Freddie was there, but every girl lined up on the stage stared back at her with a blank expression.

Well, everyone except Ally, Alice's daughter, who was staring with great fascination at something on the ceiling of the chapel. Freddie followed her gaze to see what Ally was so mesmerized by, but all she saw was a boring old ceiling. Ally was known around Auradon for being a bit of a daydreamer. Freddie guessed it must be because she had grown up hearing her mom's stories about Wonderland.

"I'm here to audition," Freddie said.

Audrey laughed. "Audition? We're the Auradonnas. We don't hold *auditions*. You have to be invited to join this group."

"But the sign. In the banquet hall," Freddie argued.

Audrey huffed, clearly growing impatient. "What sign?"

Freddie felt frustration rising in her. She was not going to be pushed around by a girl whose mother had been raised by fairies. She stood her ground. "It said there were auditions being held today at three o'clock. It's now three o'clock."

"Technically," someone said in a small voice, and Freddie saw Jane, Fairy Godmother's daughter, take a minuscule step forward, "it's three-oh-two."

"Be quiet, Jane," Audrey snapped, and Jane meekly ducked back into the line.

Audrey turned her stare back on Freddie. "I don't know what voodoo spell you're trying to cast on me right now but—"

"I'm not casting any voodoo spells on you," Freddie interrupted, putting her hands on her hips and glaring at Audrey. "I know the rules." Then, under her breath, she added, "But I'd really love to turn you into a slug right now."

"Well, anyway," Audrey went on, giving her hair

a toss, "there are no auditions. Do any of you know about any auditions?" She quickly glanced back at the group members, who were all silent and completely still, and then returned her attention to Freddie. "See? No auditions."

"Auditions?" Ally said with her posh British accent, suddenly coming out of her daydream and joining the conversation for the first time. "Is someone here to audition? Oh, splendid! I was hoping people would show. I put up a sign in the banquet hall."

Audrey reeled on Ally. "You did what?"

Ally suddenly looked a lot less confident. "Our final competition song is feeling a little stale," she said, fidgeting with her blue-and-white dress. "I just thought maybe we should bring in some fresh voices."

"But we're a four-part harmony," Audrey said through gritted teeth. "And we have *twelve* members. Three singers per part. If we added a thirteenth member, everything would be out of balance."

"Not if we—" Ally started.

But Audrey promptly cut her off. "And besides, you really shouldn't be holding auditions without checking with me first."

"I am the captain of the Auradonnas," Ally reminded

her. But there was very little conviction in her voice. "I have the right to let anyone I want into the group."

Audrey's whole body stiffened. Freddie covered her mouth with her hand to keep from laughing. Thank badness, Ally seemed to be on Freddie's side. She might be Freddie's only shot at getting into the group. And it was nice to see someone finally standing up to Audrey.

For a good five seconds, Audrey seemed to fumble for something to say. Her mouth kept opening and then closing again. Freddie thought she looked like a dying fish, which only made her want to laugh more.

Then, finally, Audrey blurted, "Yes, but you want to be a *fair* captain, don't you?"

"Of course," Ally said, clearly unsure of where Audrey was going with that.

"So you should at least ask everyone what they think before making decisions. You don't want to be seen as an evil monarch like the Queen of Hearts, do you?"

Ally seemed to shrink as she shook her head. "Oh, dear me, no."

Audrey stepped back to address the line of girls. "Very well, then. All in favor of allowing Freddie into the group?"

Ally tentatively raised her hand. She was the only

one. Everyone else looked at Audrey with almost frightened expressions and kept their hands at their sides.

Audrey turned back to Freddie and crossed her arms. "There you go. Thanks for coming by to audition."

Freddie's mouth fell open. "But you didn't even hear me sing!"

"We've heard you sing," Audrey said dismissively. "And we just think you're more of a soloist. You know, an *independent* singer. You don't really have the right voice to sing in a *group*. Sorry!" She flashed Freddie a fake smile and then returned to her position in line. "Okay, everyone, let's start from the top."

As the Auradonnas launched back into their competition song, Freddie looked hopefully at Ally, but Ally wouldn't meet her eye. With a mix of disappointment and outrage, Freddie turned and walked out of the chapel, accompanied by twelve bright and cheerful voices singing in perfect four-part harmony.

DISCARDED

I should've known those girls would never
let a VK into their precious group.

Freddie stared at her own shadow on the sidewalk as she
stomped back across campus. The sun was low at her
back, so her shadow walked tall and long in front of her,
and Freddie's tiny purple top hat with the single peacock
feather made the shape of it look like a bird resting atop
a pole.

"How dare Audrey ice me out like that!" she ranted
to the shadow.

She'd always spoken to her shadow, ever since she was
a little girl. It was what you did in the Facilier family.
And right then it seemed like her shadow was her only
friend.

"I'm a good singer!" she went on. "Maybe even the

best singer at Auradon Prep! And I *can* sing in a group. I can harmonize! I just need an opportunity to prove myself. But how am I ever going to do that when Audrey won't even let me audition?"

The shadow didn't respond. It never did. But Freddie didn't need its advice. She already knew the answer to her question.

Her best chance of getting into the Auradonnas was with Ally. That was obvious. The problem was getting Ally to stand up to Audrey. Ally was captain of the group and yet she let Audrey make all the decisions. Why was Ally (and everyone else at that school) so afraid of that intolerable pretty pink princess?

Audrey wouldn't last an hour on the Isle of the Lost.

It was on days like those that Freddie really wished she had some of her dad's magic. Her father, the once-great Dr. Facilier, would never have put up with that. He would have cast a voodoo spell on Audrey ages earlier.

But Freddie had never learned the great voodoo arts. Magic was forbidden on the Isle of the Lost, where she had grown up, so her father had never had a chance to teach her. Her father had given her a pack of Shadow Cards for her birthday, but of course they didn't work on the island, so she'd just stashed them somewhere and forgotten about them.

"Are you all right?" someone asked, interrupting Freddie's thoughts. She looked up to see Mal and Evie standing in front of Mal's open locker door. Evie, who was the one who had asked the question, was looking at Freddie, but Mal was turned toward her locker, seemingly searching for something.

Ever since Freddie and CJ had snuck out of Auradon Prep a few weeks earlier and gone on a wild adventure, Mal had seemed distant toward Freddie.

Freddie had assumed the other VKs would instantly welcome her into their little group as soon as she arrived in Auradon. But lately it seemed like Mal was avoiding her, and although Evie was always nice to her, she was usually busy with all her new clubs and classes.

"You seem a little stressed out," Evie went on. "You should try to relax. Stress is horrible for your complexion."

"So is Audrey," Freddie mumbled.

Evie laughed. "Don't let Audrey get to you."

"Easy for you to say," Freddie replied. "She happens to *like* you."

"She tolerates us," Evie said, correcting her, as she gestured between Mal and herself. "I wouldn't say she likes us."

"Don't worry, the feeling is mutual," Mal said with

a dark laugh, and for a moment, Freddie wondered if the joke was a sign that Mal was opening up a bit. But then Mal shut her locker door and said, "I gotta go help Ben work on his tour speech. See you later, Evie." Then she rushed off, not even bothering to say another word to Freddie.

Lately Mal had been preoccupied, helping King Ben, her boyfriend, prepare for some big upcoming royal tour of Auradon. He was going to visit all the towns in the kingdom and give important speeches. Apparently, it was a pretty big deal, as he was a new king and he had to make a good impression on his subjects.

"Don't worry about her," Evie said after Mal had left, clearly reading Freddie's conflicted expression. "Mal's just stressed out about the tour."

"She's mad at me. I can feel it."

"She's not *mad*," Evie said cautiously. "She's just . . . being extra careful. She can't afford to get in trouble right now. She has to make a good impression. As Ben's girlfriend."

Freddie pretended to be shocked. "*Me* get someone in trouble? Where could you possibly have gotten such an outrageous idea?"

Evie raised an eyebrow and they both laughed.

It felt good. Freddie hadn't really laughed with

anyone since she and CJ had come back from their treasure chase. But then, a second later, Freddie remembered what had just happened in the chapel, and her smile instantly fell.

"What's wrong?" Evie asked.

Freddie sighed. "I just thought things would be easier here than on the Isle of the Lost."

"And they're not?"

Freddie scoffed. "Not really. I mean, Audrey is basically a villain in a pink dress. She could give your mother a run for her money."

"Don't let her hear you say that."

"Who? Audrey? Or your mother?"

Evie snickered. "Both."

Evie took her handheld mirror out of her bag and used it to reapply her bright red lipstick. Technically, the mirror was magic, just like the one her mom, the Evil Queen, had. But Freddie knew Evie rarely used the magic part anymore. Magic was frowned upon in Auradon, and in addition to being one of the smartest kids in the school, Evie had become quite the rule follower lately.

"Hey," Freddie said, motioning toward the dorm. "Wanna come to my room and hang out? We can make curse dolls of Audrey."

Evie giggled, putting the mirror back into her bag. "As fun as that sounds, I'm late to my sewing club. We're making all of the costumes for Ben's entourage for the tour! But maybe later?"

Freddie slouched. "Sure," she replied, trying not to sound as disappointed as she felt. "Maybe later."

I miss CJ, Freddie thought, heading into the dorm.

As she climbed the stairs to her room, she wondered if it had been a mistake to stay there while CJ was off pillaging and plundering on the high seas. Maybe she should have set sail with her best friend after all.

She only wanted to be at Auradon Prep so she could sing. And so far, that was proving to be much more difficult than she'd thought it would.

When she reached her dorm room, she collapsed onto her bed with a sigh and stared at the empty bed where CJ had slept during the week she'd stowed away there, wreaking havoc on the school with all her pranks. The fake pirate ship sail CJ had fashioned out of a sheet was still strung across the four posts of the bed.

Freddie smiled at the memory of their first day there, when CJ had come in with her red pirate coat and crocodile-skin boots, ranting about how much she hated the decorations.

But Freddie's reverie was interrupted a moment later by a knock at the door. "Mail delivery!" a girl said sarcastically from the hallway.

Confused, Freddie frowned at the door.

Mail delivery?

She never got mail. Who would send it to her? Everyone she knew was trapped on the Isle of the Lost without any way of communicating with the rest of the kingdom. And even if they could communicate, villains weren't exactly known for writing letters.

She scooted off the bed and opened the door to find Jordan standing in the hallway in her dramatic blue harem pants and gold jacket. Jordan was the Genie's daughter, an AK, but Freddie didn't mind her too much. For an AK, she was actually pretty cool. She was snarky and always quick to tell off anyone who got in her face. But she was usually too busy with her überpopular Web show to bother much with Freddie.

"This was delivered for you while you were gone," Jordan said dismissively, gesturing to a strange object in her hand. "Please take it. It *really* doesn't go with the lamp decor of my bedroom."

Freddie tilted her head to get a better look at what Jordan was holding.

What is that? she thought. *It almost looks like a . . .*

"Duh, it's a bottle," Jordan snapped, shoving it into Freddie's hands. "And *not* the 'genie in a bottle' kind of bottle. The other, *boring* kind of bottle."

"Yeah, but why was it delivered to me?" Freddie asked.

"I don't know," Jordan said impatiently. "I'm not a messenger service." Then she spun on her gold heels and disappeared down the hallway.

Freddie chuckled. She liked that girl more and more every day.

Freddie closed the door and carried the bottle to her bed to examine it more closely. It was made out of a thick dark glass and had a cork stuffed into the opening. The glass was opaque, but she could tell by shaking the bottle that there was something inside.

A message?

In a bottle?

Who would send me a message in a . . .

But before she even had a chance to finish the thought, the answer became obvious to her.

"CJ!" she said, eagerly removing the cork and shaking out the contents. A small rolled-up piece of paper fell onto her bedspread. Freddie eagerly unfurled the message and read her best friend's messy handwriting.

Freddster!

What's up, old chum? I'm writing you this message from the mighty seven seas! Well, one of them, anyway. I was halfway across the ocean when I realized I forgot to tell you about the little gift I left for you. I brought it over from the Isle of the Lost because I thought it might come in handy at some point, but then I buried it under the bleachers of the tourney field and completely forgot about it. By the way, have you figured out how tourney is played yet?

Anyway, just in case you need a little (wink, wink) help, it's there waiting for you.

Have fun in Pretty Pretty Princess Land! Don't let those ruffle queens change you too much, okay? And remember, if you ever change your mind, I could always use a first mate on the ship. Just kidding. Partners for reals. For life.

Insincerely,

CJ

Freddie was so overjoyed by the message she could hardly contain herself. She jumped off the bed and ran out of her dorm room, not even bothering to shut the door behind her.

By the time she reached the tourney field, she was out of breath again, but she didn't care. She was far too excited to find out what CJ had left for her. If her friend had taken the time not only to hide the gift but also to send Freddie a message about it, then it was probably something really evil.

And Freddie could use a little evil in her life right then.

The Fighting Knights tourney team was in the middle of practice when she slyly made her way to the bleachers. As usual, Jay, Jafar's son, was in command of the entire field, running the ball all the way to the goal without being tackled once. Meanwhile, Carlos, Cruella De Vil's son, who was decidedly *less* skilled at tourney, stood off to the side with his scruffy little dog, Dude, watching the action with a sour expression on his face.

Freddie felt kind of sorry for Carlos. Jay was always getting all the attention on the tourney field. She often forgot Carlos was even *on* the team.

Before anyone could notice her, Freddie ducked under the bleachers and started to look around. But she had no idea *where* CJ could have buried the gift. The bleachers were huge. She could be digging all night.

Then, after walking around for about five minutes,

she noticed something on the ground under her feet, and her mouth curved into a knowing smile.

Someone had drawn a very faint skull and cross-bones in the dirt.

"X marks the spot," Freddie whispered with a smirk.

She dropped to her knees and started digging. After a while it felt like she had been digging forever. Her hands were getting tired, her fingernails were caked with dirt, and she'd ripped a hole in her purple tights. For a moment, surrounded by all the mess, she felt almost like she was back on the Isle of the Lost.

Then her hands made contact with something hard. Eagerly, Freddie dug faster until she had completely uncovered a small wooden box. She tried to open the lid but it was locked. Then she noticed the small keyhole in the front.

She held up the box to examine the lock.

"*Psh.* Child's play," she mumbled.

Freddie had been picking locks since she was a little girl. She could pick this lock in her sleep—something CJ definitely would have known.

Careful to keep the box hidden, Freddie carried it back to her dorm room and rummaged around in her drawers until she found a hairpin. She straightened it out and inserted it into the lock, wiggling until the mechanism disengaged and she heard a soft click.

Then she slowly opened the lid and let out a gasp when she saw what CJ had placed inside.

Lying in the wooden box was her old deck of Shadow Cards! They were the ones her father had given her on her tenth birthday. They were supposed to show you the path to your deepest desire, but they'd never worked on the Isle of the Lost, where magic was banned, so she'd never been able to test them out.

But Freddie knew they would certainly work in Auradon.

She couldn't help laughing. It was as though her best friend knew exactly what she needed exactly *when* she needed it.

And right then, more than anything, Freddie definitely needed a little magic.

SUITED

Dad told me I'd be able to use the cards someday. And that day is today.

I mean, how hard could it be?

Freddie fanned the cards out on her bed and stared at the creepy, shadowy images depicted on their faces. Slithering snakes, and horned monsters, and a half man, half beast. She grinned wildly. She hadn't seen the cards in years; it was like a piece of her childhood was coming back to her.

Each card was different but fascinating in its own way. Just looking at the images on the cards made something light up inside Freddie. Like a flame. A long-lost power.

She could almost *feel* the magic in the cards come to life.

She bit her lip and tried to remember everything her father had told her over the years about Shadow Cards. She knew they could tell you where to go and what to do to find your deepest desire. But how did they work? What was she supposed to do with them? Just shuffle and pick one?

It was worth a shot.

She gathered up the cards, gave them a quick shuffle, and spread them out again, this time facedown so all the creepy images were hidden.

She took a deep breath and spoke as clearly as possible.

"How do I get into the Auradonnas?"

Then she passed her hand over each card, waiting for something to happen. A feeling? A sense? A pull?

But she felt nothing. That small flicker that had come over her when she first spread out the deck was suddenly gone.

She grabbed one of the cards at random and turned it over, frowning at the image.

It was a picture of a pig sleeping in mud.

Not super helpful.

What was she supposed to do with that?

With a frustrated sigh, she gathered up the cards again. She was definitely missing something, missing a step. But what?

And how would she ever figure it out? It wasn't like she could walk up to Headmistress Fairy Godmother— or any of the faculty there—and say, "Hey! Can you teach me how to use these black magic Shadow Cards that my villainous father gave me?"

They'd kick her out for sure. And then she'd never get to be Auradon's most famous jazz singer.

She shuffled the cards twice and then fanned them again, facedown, as she tried to think of what to do.

Then she noticed what was on the *back side* of the cards. She hadn't really looked closely at them before. On the front side, all the cards were different, but on the back they all had the same design: a swirling gold border with a strange-looking symbol in the center. As she leaned in to get a closer look, she realized the symbol was actually the outline of two hands facing away from each other. In the palm of each hand was a large black eye.

"What does that mean?" Freddie asked her shadow, which was seated beside her on the bed, formed by the soft light of her bedside lamp. "A hand with an eye in it? Like the hand can see something? Like it knows something?"

The thought made her (and her shadow) jump as a memory flooded back to her. The nursery rhyme from her childhood! The one her father used to sing to her when she couldn't fall asleep.

Masters of the Shadow Land,
I call upon your knowing hand.
I offer you this sinner's song
To guide the path I walk upon.

Maybe it wasn't a nursery rhyme. Maybe it was some kind of shadow spell!

Excitement burst inside Freddie's chest as she quickly reshuffled the cards and spread them out again on her comforter. She closed her eyes, and her hand hovered a few inches above them as she carefully recited the rhyme. "*Masters of the Shadow Land, I call upon your knowing hand. I offer you this sinner's song, to guide the path I walk upon.*"

Freddie opened her eyes to witness an incredible sight. Her shadow was no longer just a shadow. It was moving—all on its own! It seemed to be shriveling up, becoming smaller and smaller, until it was just a long, squiggly line, like a snake made of smoke.

Then the snake slithered along the surface of her bed. Freddie fought the urge to jump back.

"Where are you going?" she asked it.

The answer soon became obvious as the shadow snake veered left and headed straight for the center of her bed.

The cards! Freddie thought with sudden realization.

Her shadow was moving toward the cards!

As soon as it reached them, Freddie felt the cards awaken. It was like a buzz of electricity running through her. Like her own shadow had given the cards life.

The snake proceeded to slither across the back side of each card, touching them one by one.

Freddie sucked in a breath and waited. She wasn't sure what she was supposed to do next, but it became evident when the shadow snake formed a question mark across the backs of the cards.

It was time to get the answer she needed.

Freddie cleared her throat and asked, "How do I get into the Auradonnas?"

The cards responded quickly. Freddie let out a tiny gasp as she watched a bouncing ball of purple light materialize over the deck and jump from card to card before finally coming to rest on a single one near the middle of the deck. The card glowed in response, as though absorbing the light right into its surface.

With her heart hammering, Freddie reached out and flipped over the card.

On the front was a picture of a street. Freddie frowned in confusion. She didn't recognize the street and there were no street signs or landmarks to guide her.

"Am I supposed to *go* to that street?" she asked the card. "But how do I know where it is?"

Then, suddenly, the picture on the card came to life. The street started to move. It was as though she were floating above the road, traveling down it, until she started to recognize some familiar landmarks.

A castle.

A chapel.

A field.

It's Auradon Prep! Freddie realized. *That's the tourney field! I was just there.*

The moving picture crossed the field before coming to a stop outside a small store, which Freddie immediately recognized as the Mad for Tea tea shop. She had visited it several times with Mal, Evie, and the gang.

She stared intently at the card, waiting for it to reveal more, but the image was frozen on the tea shop.

Freddie was thoroughly confused.

A tea shop?

How is that supposed to help me get into the Auradonnas?

Almost as soon as the question entered her head, she remembered something about the tea shop: it was owned by Ally's parents.

And Ally was the captain of the Auradonnas.

Freddie sat up straighter and stared at the picture again.

Could the card really be telling her to go there? Maybe to try to convince Ally to let her into the group. But that seemed impossible. Ally was too scared of Audrey. She would never stand up to her.

But Freddie knew from listening to her father talk about his lost profession as the shadow man that Shadow Cards never lied. They could be tricky when they wanted to be, but they always told the truth—which meant Freddie had to listen to them if she wanted to get what she asked for.

Freddie gathered up the cards and retied the string around them. As soon as she did so, she felt her shadow slide back into place beside her, like someone had draped a cold blanket around her. She hid the deck safely in the pocket of her dress. She knew she'd have to be very careful with the cards. They were dark. And they were magic. If Fairy Godmother found out she had them, she'd take them away instantly and maybe even expel Freddie for having them.

That meant she would have to keep the cards to herself.

It would be her little secret.

Well, hers and CJ's, obviously.

Freddie smiled at the thought of sharing a secret with her best friend, even though she was hundreds—maybe even thousands—of miles away. It made Freddie feel closer to her somehow.

"Wow," she commented to her shadow as they both stood up. "What a cheesy thought!"

Maybe CJ is right. Maybe Auradon Prep really is getting to me.

Freddie walked to the dresser and stared hard at her reflection in the mirror for a long minute. She certainly didn't *look* any less villainous than she remembered, but that was the thing about change: it happened so gradually you never could really tell until it was too late.

Next thing I know, I'm going to start twirling and whistling while I work.

Freddie shuddered. She would *not* let that happen. Going to Auradon Prep and wanting to sing a cappella did *not* make her an AK. She was still a VK through and through.

She could be a villain *and* like to sing catchy, upbeat songs. She would just be a different *kind* of villain. A new generation of villain. But still rotten to the core.

Obviously.

However, just to be on the safe side, Freddie spent the next few minutes twisting her face into a series of ferocious scowls in the mirror.

Much better, she thought.

As Freddie headed out of the dorm, her shadow following her obediently, she patted the pocket of her dress, double-checking to make sure her Shadow Cards were still safely hidden inside. She had no idea what would be waiting for her when she got to the tea shop, but she wanted to be ready.

JUST DEAL

*Umm . . . what am I going
to do at a tea shop?*

*Do they sell some kind of magical scone that
will get me into the Auradonnas?*

When Freddie arrived at the Mad for Tea shop, the place
was so unrecognizable she almost walked back out to check
the sign on the door. The whole shop had been completely
transformed. There were ticking pocket watches on every
table, a large black-and-white checkered rug covering the
floor, massive fake mushrooms towering in the corners
like trees, and giant neon caterpillars decorating the walls.

Ally was sitting on a couch in the middle of everything, frowning down at her phone.

"Are you having a party?" Freddie asked, confused.

"No!" Ally wailed. She lifted her head to look at Freddie, and Freddie could see that she'd been crying. Her eyes were red and puffy, and her cheeks were streaked with tears.

Freddie glanced around the unrecognizable tea shop again. "Then what is all of this?"

"A party!" Ally said as though it were obvious.

Freddie scowled. "But I thought you just said—"

"I'm decorating for a fund-raising party that's tomorrow night," Ally began, new tears quickly filling her eyes. "For the Auradonnas. We need new costumes for our finale song, and Mum said I could hold the fund-raiser here at the tea shop while she was on vacation. I sent out tons of ZapChats but barely anyone's responded!" She held out her phone as though offering proof.

Freddie's eyebrows knit together. "There's a fund-raising party tomorrow night?"

Ally threw up her hands. "Exactly! It's like no one even knows about it! Audrey is going to be livid when she finds out I botched up this party and we have no RSVPs. How will we ever raise enough money for our costumes if no one comes? And if we don't have new costumes, we won't impress the judges, and then the Sword in the Tone will win and take our championship title away from us!"

Freddie fought the urge to roll her eyes. She'd always known Ally to be a little bit on the peculiar side, but it seemed she was also dramatic. "I think you might be overreacting," Freddie said, trying to sound diplomatic. She knew if she was going to convince Ally to let her into the Auradonnas, she had to be *nice*—as much as she despised that word. But she certainly wasn't going to talk her way into the Auradonnas by being herself.

"I'm not overreacting!" Ally argued. Then, suddenly, her eyes got very wide and panicked, and she shouted, "No! Stop! Bad! Bad! You'll be sick in the morning!"

Freddie was thoroughly confused. She blinked at Ally, who seemed to be staring right at her. "Who are you talking to?" Freddie asked.

"Dino," Ally said. "He's being naughty again."

Freddie glanced behind her but saw nothing. "Uh, is Dino *real* or just your imagination?"

Ally scoffed and stood up, then walked to the table of cakes, pies, and cookies behind Freddie. "Of course Dino's real." She grabbed the orange-and-white cat who was sneaking toward one of the desserts.

"He keeps trying to eat all the whipped honey butter," Ally explained, returning to the couch and holding Dino in her arms. "I told him not to, but sometimes he does it anyway. I've talked to him countless times about controlling his impulses, but he just doesn't listen. I haven't a clue why."

"Um, maybe because he's a cat?" Freddie suggested.

Ally shook her head. "No, that's not it."

Freddie squinted at her.

Forget that we're from the Isle of the Lost. This girl lives on her own planet.

Ally scratched the cat between the ears and glanced around the tea shop with a heavy sigh. "This is such a shame. I worked so hard on this party. I did a whole Wonderland theme and everything. And now no one will even see it."

Freddie peered at the strange decorations. "Is that what this is? I thought it was some kind of caterpillar disco."

That was apparently the wrong thing to say, because Ally immediately started crying again—this time even harder. Freddie worried if she didn't stop soon, they *both* might drown in all those tears.

Freddie stood there, fidgeting awkwardly. She wasn't sure what to say. She didn't have much experience consoling people. Not many people cried on the Isle of the Lost. At least not in public. Plus, Freddie's father had never been very tender with her while she was growing up. When she was little and she would scrape her knee and tears would start to well in her eyes, her father would just pick her up, dust off the scraped knee, and say, "Real villains don't cry."

But now Ally was staring at Freddie with those weepy eyes like she was expecting her to say something kind and reassuring. Maybe that was what you did when you saw someone crying in Auradon: you comforted them.

Freddie sighed and sat down in the chair next to Ally, trying to remember what she'd seen the AKs do in situations like that. She vaguely remembered some back patting. Freddie reached out and patted Ally awkwardly on the shoulder with the back of her hand. She felt ridiculous.

"Uh," Freddie said, fumbling for something to say. "It's okay. Don't cry. Things could be a lot worse."

Strangely, that seemed to work. Ally sniffled and looked at Freddie with her big blue eyes full of tears. "They could?"

Freddie shrugged. "Sure. I mean, I could think of tons of things worse than no one RSVPing to a party."

"Like what?" Ally asked, looking curious.

Freddie pursed her lips, trying to recall all the bedtime stories her father used to tell her at night. "Well, let's see. You could fall into a swamp and get bitten by a poisonous snake. You could wake up in the morning to find your head has been shrunk. Your shadow could steal all of your stuff in the middle of the night. Or!" she added with sudden inspiration as she glanced at the cat in Ally's lap. "Your mom's cat could get run over by a truck!"

Ally's eyes widened and tears started to well up again. "Oh, dear. Poor Dino!" She nuzzled her face in the cat's fur. "I won't let that happen, Dino. I promise!"

And she was off again, sobbing relentlessly.

Okay, maybe Freddie had gone a bit too far with the last one.

"Look," Freddie said, quickly losing patience with all the weepiness. "Instead of sitting around crying about it, why don't you try to figure out ways to get people to come?"

Ally sniffled and looked up at Freddie with wide tear-rimmed eyes. "Like what?"

Freddie shrugged. "I don't know. Maybe you could—"

"You're right!" Ally cried out suddenly, scaring both Freddie and the cat. The cat screeched and leapt off her lap, then scurried under the table. "We need to advertise! We need to put up flyers everywhere. We'll design a really nice poster with a picture of a caterpillar eating a piece of cake, or a piece of cake drinking a cup of tea. Or we'll draw a mushroom—"

"Hold up," Freddie said, interrupting her. "What do you mean 'we'?"

Ally looked like she didn't understand the question. "You'll help, won't you? Isn't that why you came by?"

"No," Freddie replied. "I came by because . . ." Her voice trailed off as she remembered the reason she was there: to get into the Auradonnas. Was that what the Shadow Cards were telling her to do? Help Ally put up a bunch of flyers for a party? How would *that* get her into the Auradonnas?

Freddie bit her lip as she considered her next words carefully.

Her father had taught her that when you wanted something from someone, the only way to guarantee you'd get it was to convince them they needed *you* more than you needed *them*.

So what did Ally *need* from Freddie that she couldn't get from anyone else?

Freddie glanced around the tea shop and suddenly caught sight of her shadow sitting next to her on the couch. From the way the light overhead was casting it, her shadow looked like it was reaching for something in Freddie's pocket.

Reaching for . . .

The Shadow Cards!

"Oh!" Freddie said. "Of course!"

How could it have taken her that long to realize? That was why the Shadow Cards had sent her there. That was how she was going to get into the Auradonnas. It was so simple yet so *brilliant* she almost pulled out the cards and kissed them right then and there.

"What?" Ally asked, staring at Freddie with a curious expression. "What is it? Do you have a better idea than the caterpillar eating a piece of cake?"

"Yes," Freddie said smugly. "I have a *much* better idea."

Ally looked skeptical. "You do?"

Freddie nodded, gaining confidence by the second. "Yes, I do."

"What?"

It was almost as though, right then, Freddie could feel the cards pulsing in her pocket, the dark spirits inside them begging to be let out, coaxing her on, whispering, *"Yes. Use us. We can help."*

Freddie rubbed her hands together, feeling more powerful than she had in a very long time. "Let's make a deal, shall we?"

CARD TRICK

I love when a plan comes together.

Ally is about to find out what makes me
the daughter of the shadow man.

"What are they?" Ally asked, gaping at the deck of cards
Freddie had just pulled out of her pocket.

"They're called Shadow Cards and they will answer
any question you ask."

"Ooh," Ally said. "Can I touch them?" She reached
out her finger toward the deck.

Freddie yanked the cards out of Ally's reach. "Absolutely not. Only the shadow princess can touch the cards."

"Shadow princess?" Ally repeated doubtfully.

Freddie pursed her lips. "You're right. It doesn't have
the right ring, does it? I'll work on my title later. First

things first." Freddie gave the cards a quick shuffle and fanned them out on the table in front of them, front side down.

Ally leaned forward and studied the picture that was on the back of the cards: two open palms with an eye in the center of each.

"What curious-looking flowers," Ally mused.

Freddie huffed. "They're not flowers. They're—You know what? Never mind. Let's just get on with it. All you have to do is ask the cards what you want and they'll tell you how to get it."

Ally was clearly skeptical. "That's it?"

Freddie nodded. "That's it."

"Are they even allowed at Auradon Prep?"

Freddie's head teetered. "Not *technically*. But if you want to get people to this fund-raiser and raise enough money to buy the costumes, the cards will help."

Ally bit her lip and stared down at the Shadow Cards, obviously contemplating her choices. "I don't know. I don't want to get in trouble for using magic."

Freddie sighed dramatically and scooped up the cards. "That's fine," she said, slipping easily into her smooth "velvet voice." That was the voice she used when she was trying to talk someone into something. It was a skill she had learned from her father. "I get it. You don't want to use magic. You don't want to get in trouble. It's too bad, though. It's obvious this would have been an amazing party. And you would have been an *amazing* hostess." She made a show of glancing around the tea shop and admiring all the decorations. "I can almost see it now. Everyone laughing and eating those delicious cakes and pies, drinking cups of steaming hot tea, saying things like, 'Oh, Ally! This scone is simply divine! You sure know how to throw a party.'"

Freddie snuck a look at Ally. She was gazing longingly at the dessert table, obviously imagining exactly what Freddie was describing. The velvet voice was working. Then again, it rarely failed.

"It's a pity," Freddie went on with a fake sigh. "It really would have been wonderful. Or should I say Wonder-*land*ful?" She stood up and slipped the deck of cards into her pocket. "Oh, well. I'm sure you'll figure out another way to raise money for the costumes. Good luck!"

Freddie started to walk away, but she barely got two steps toward the door before she heard Ally cry out, "Wait!"

Freddie smiled and turned around.

"How fast do the cards work?" Ally asked.

Freddie thought back to what had happened in her dorm room: how the cards had guided her to that tea shop and within minutes she had understood what she had to do. "Almost instantly."

Ally looked torn. She chewed on her bottom lip. "Okay, I'll do it."

Freddie sat back down and pulled the cards from her pocket again, then shuffled them. "Great. Let's talk about payment."

Ally looked confused. "Payment?"

"For my services," Freddie clarified. "You can't receive a favor from the shadow *sorceress* without paying some kind of price in return."

Ally cocked her head pensively. "Shadow sorceress?"

Freddie tried again. "Shadow enchantress?"

"Nope."

Freddie groaned. "I'll get there."

"What kind of price are we talking about?"

Freddie smirked. "Not much, really. A steal of a deal, if you ask me. I help you get people to this fund-raiser and you get me into the Auradonnas."

Ally's reaction was easy to read. She clearly was not comfortable with that. "Oh, I don't know. That's not something I can just promise."

"You *are* the captain, right?" Freddie asked.

"Yes, but—"

"So you *do* have final say in who gets into the group."

"Of course, but—"

Freddie shrugged. "Then I don't see what the problem is."

Ally hesitated. "You do have a great voice. It's just that Audrey—"

"Hey, do you want to get those new costumes or not?" Freddie was starting to lose patience.

Ally sighed. "Okay, okay. I'll do it. I'll get you into the Auradonnas *if* I raise enough money to buy the costumes."

Freddie held out her hand. Ally just stared at it like she'd never seen a hand before.

Freddie rolled her eyes. "We have to shake on it."

"Oh! Right. Of course." She extended her hand toward Freddie.

And the deal was sealed.

Freddie waved her hands majestically over the cards spread out on the table. Almost instantly, she could feel the shadow spirits awaken within them, fill them with life. Her whole body tingled as her own shadow readied itself.

"Masters of the Shadow Land," Freddie began to chant, "I call upon your knowing hand."

"Ooh!" Ally cried out excitedly. "Masters of the Shadow Land! Cool!"

Freddie shot her a look. Ally shrunk down in her chair. "Sorry! I get a little overexcited about things."

"Really? I hadn't noticed," Freddie mumbled sarcastically.

Ally giggled.

Freddie cleared her throat and began again, floating her hand a few inches above the face-down cards.

"Masters of the Shadow Land, I call upon your knowing hand. I offer you this sinner's song, to guide the path she walks upon."

Freddie felt her shadow start to contract again, getting thinner and thinner, until it had completely transformed into the smoky black snake. She expected Ally to yelp at the sight of it and possibly run away, but she didn't. Ally just watched the process with great fascination, her blue eyes wide and full of wonder.

The dark, slithering shadow snake glided over and around the cards before finally forming the question mark.

"Go ahead," Freddie said to Ally. "Ask them what you want."

Ally glanced uneasily from the cards to Freddie and then asked in a whisper, "Do I have to say a chant, too?"

"No," Freddie replied. "You just have to ask a question. And you don't have to whisper."

"Oh," Ally whispered, and then caught herself. "Oh," she said again at a normal volume. "Right, then." She turned her attention to the cards and Freddie's transformed shadow. "Um. Hello there, creepy magic cards. I love the shadow snake thing. Very nice touch."

Freddie rolled her eyes again. "What are you doing?"

Ally looked insulted. "I'm complimenting the cards."

"You don't have to compliment them."

"It can't hurt, can it? Mum says everyone appreciates good manners."

"Fine," Freddie huffed. "Go ahead. Buy them a cup of tea if you must. Just get on with it."

Ally swallowed and continued addressing the cards. "Right, then. Where were we? Oh, right, you are so very lovely and wise and . . . wicked!" She beamed up at Freddie, as if expecting some kind of award for using the word *wicked*.

Freddie flashed a fake smile. "Good one."

"So," Ally went on, "I was just wondering, if you wouldn't mind, of course, if you would kindly tell me how to get people to come to my fund-raiser." She stopped and then, as though remembering, quickly added, "Thank you very much."

The shadow snake converged into a ball of purple light, which bounced over the cards before slowing to a stop. Then the light seemed to be pondering its next move. It hovered tentatively between two cards.

Ally looked anxiously at Freddie. "What's happening?"

"Shhh. The cards are thinking."

Both girls stared in awe at the light as it finally made a decision and sank into its chosen card, which pulsated wildly in response.

"Go ahead," Freddie said, encouraging Ally. "Pick it. See what it says."

Hesitantly, Ally reached out and plucked the glowing card. She flipped it over on the table so both girls could see.

On the face of the card was a picture of a large stone castle with blue and yellow flags hanging from the turrets.

Ally leapt out of her chair in excitement. "That's the dorm of Auradon Prep!" Then her thoughts seemed to catch up to her and her excitement melted into confusion. "Wait, how does that help me get people to my party?"

Freddie caught her arm and pulled her back down. "Just wait. *Watch.*"

"Watch what?" Ally asked, glancing at the card. "I don't—" But her words were cut off when the picture on the card suddenly came to life. Just as the other one had done in response to Freddie's question, the image started to move, and soon the girls were no longer looking at the front of the Auradon Prep dormitory. The image traveled through the entrance of the castle and up the curving staircase to the second floor.

"What's it doing?" Ally asked.

"It's telling us what to do."

The moving picture on the card traveled down a long corridor before finally stopping at a door, which Freddie instantly recognized as the entrance to Evie and Mal's dorm room. She felt her throat constrict at the memory of Mal ignoring her that afternoon at the lockers. Freddie wished she could figure out a way to get Mal on her side again.

"I don't understand," Ally said, interrupting Freddie's thoughts. "Why'd it stop?"

Freddie blinked and focused on the Shadow Card in front of her. The image was frozen on the door to Mal and Evie's room.

"That's where you need to go to find what you're looking for," Freddie said.

"But why? How am I going to get people to my party by going to Mal and Evie's room?"

Freddie shrugged. "I guess you'll find out when you get there."

"*Me?*" Ally asked, sounding surprised. "Aren't you coming with me?"

Freddie gathered up the cards and returned them to her pocket. "Nah. I think my work here is done."

Ally looked like she was going to cry again. "Oh, but you can't make me go on my own! You *have* to come with me. Mal still terrifies me a little, and I don't think Evie likes me quite much."

"Uh, I don't *have* to do anything."

Ally stomped her foot. "I won't let you into the Auradonnas unless you come with me."

That made Freddie angry. She did *not* like being threatened. She crossed her arms over her chest. "That was not our deal."

"That's right," Ally said, challenging her. "Our deal was that I will only let you into the group if we raise enough money for the costumes. So it's in your best interest to help me do that."

Freddie hated to admit it, but Ally was right. That *was* what they had shaken on. But hanging out with Ally was certainly *not* how Freddie imagined spending her evening.

HELPING HAND?

Desperate times call for evil measures.

Hopefully I can count on my fellow VKs.

Fifteen minutes later, Ally and Freddie were standing outside Mal and Evie's closed dorm room door, taking turns peering through the keyhole.

When it was Freddie's turn to look, she was relieved to find that Mal wasn't inside. She was probably off helping Ben prepare for his royal Auradon tour. Freddie was glad she didn't have to deal with her right then. She had enough things on her plate. She didn't need to be reminded that Maleficent's daughter was barely talking to her.

Through the tiny keyhole, Freddie could see that Evie was alone in the dorm room, studying. She was reciting chemistry formulas aloud, like she was trying to commit them to memory.

"What now?" Ally whispered beside Freddie in the hallway.

To be honest, Freddie wasn't sure. She was starting to understand the mysterious Shadow Cards a little better. They didn't seem to want to tell you *exactly* what to do to get what you wanted; they just kind of pointed you in the right direction. The rest was up to you.

Like how they didn't actually tell her to use the Shadow Cards with Ally to get into the Auradonnas; they just showed her the tea shop. And now they weren't telling Ally *why* the two of them were standing in the hallway, staring though a keyhole; Freddie just knew that the answer was somewhere inside that room.

Freddie bit her lip and pressed her face harder against the doorknob, scanning the room in search of something that might give them a clue to *how* they were going to get people to attend the fund-raiser. But nothing seemed terribly obvious.

Freddie sighed and backed away from the door. "I don't know."

"You don't know?" Ally whisper-yelled. "How could you not *know*? You're the one with the magic cards!"

Freddie panicked at the mention of her cards in

that public place. She shot looks over both shoulders. "Shhh! Not so loud! Do you want the entire school to know we've been using shadow magic? Do you want Headmistress Fairy Godmother to find out?" Freddie took a deep breath and attempted to reign in her temper. "Besides," she went on, "I think the person who asks the question is supposed to interpret the answer."

Ally cocked her head, looking confused. "But how am *I* supposed to interpret the answer?"

Freddie motioned toward the keyhole. "Just look again."

Ally sighed. "Well, I suppose it's fitting. Mum did once travel through a keyhole."

Freddie had no idea what Ally was talking about. She could never tell if the girl was for real or not. So she just smiled and nodded. "Great. So take a look and see if anything catches your attention."

Ally bent down and closed one eye so she could peer through the small hole.

"What do you see?" Freddie prompted her.

"I see a dorm room," Ally said, defeated.

"Look closer," Freddie said encouragingly.

"I see Evie checking her reflection in her magic mirror. Now she's talking to the mirror," Ally reported, her face still glued to the door.

"What is she saying?" Freddie asked.

"I don't know. I can't really hear." Then Ally gasped and pulled away from the door, staring wide-eyed at Freddie. "Do you think she's asking it a question? Like a magic question? She's not supposed to do that, you know? She got in trouble for using the mirror to cheat in class."

Freddie had heard about that. It was before she came to Auradon. Evie had been asking the mirror complex science questions, and the mirror had shown her the answers. Chad Charming eventually turned her in for cheating, and Fairy Godmother made Evie promise not to use the mirror for magic anymore. But Freddie knew for a fact that Evie occasionally broke that promise.

"Have you ever asked it a question?" Ally asked curiously.

Freddie shook her head. "The mirror never worked on the Isle of the Lost."

"I would ask the mirror how to get people to my fund-raiser."

"You already asked the Shadow Cards that," Freddie pointed out.

"Yes," Ally admitted, "but so far, I'm not overly impressed with the results. I'm starting to think those cards of yours don't really work."

"Hey!" Freddie crossed her arms in defiance. "They work."

"Not very well. I mean, we've been standing out in this hallway for more than ten minutes and we still don't know why," Ally reasoned. "If we had asked Evie's mirror, we would have had an answer already. That's powerful magic. People would pay good money for that kind of immediate . . ." Ally's voice trailed off.

But Freddie barely noticed. She was still bristling from the insult to her cards. "Well, if you're *so* enamored by Evie's magic mirror, why don't you just get *her* to help you?"

"That's it!" Ally cried. "Evie's magic mirror!"

Freddie scoffed. "Fine. Do whatever you want. But don't come asking for my help again." She started to stalk off down the hallway, but Ally ran to catch up to her and pulled her to a stop. "No! You don't understand. The cards! Evie's dorm room! The mirror! Talking caterpillars, it's brilliant!"

"You're right," Freddie grumbled. "I don't understand."

"That's how we're going to get people to the tea party fund-raiser!" Ally exclaimed. "We'll host a raffle! People can buy tickets and the winner gets a chance to ask Evie's magic mirror a question!"

FACE CARD

Mirror, mirror in my hand,

Hope this party goes as planned.

It took some convincing over dinner, but Evie finally agreed to allow *one* raffle prizewinner to ask her magic mirror a question.

"Well, it *is* for a good cause," Evie said, smiling at Ally and Freddie. "And good is the new bad, right?"

"Exactly!" Ally said, and disappeared to her dorm room to send out a new ZapChat about the party.

By breakfast the next morning, kids were already talking about the fund-raiser and what question they were going to ask the mirror when they won the raffle. The RSVPs were pouring in by the minute, and Jordan even decided to feature the fund-raiser on her Web show.

"This is going to be wondrous!" Ally exclaimed as she put the finishing touches on the cake she was frosting that afternoon.

The fund-raiser was scheduled to start in less than ten minutes, and the crew—Mal, Evie, Jordan, Freddie, Lonnie, and Audrey—had come to help her finish setting up.

Everyone in the group had been assigned a task around the teahouse. Lonnie was setting up her DJ equipment in the corner; Audrey was tying satin ribbons around the flower vases; Mal and Evie were transferring iced cookies onto platters; and Freddie was lighting little tea candles in the center of each table.

"Is everything ready?" Ally asked.

"Ready," everyone responded in unison.

Freddie returned her pack of matches to the pocket of her dress. That matchbook was one of her favorite possessions. She'd taken it from the Bass Notes and Beignets jazz club she'd visited in the bayou with CJ. She liked keeping the matchbook on her because it reminded her of her dream to become a jazz singer. And every time she looked at it, she felt the dream grow stronger.

"Uh, quick question," Evie said, holding up a cookie Ally had decorated. "Why does this cookie say 'please take nourishment from me'?"

"Oh!" Ally replied with excitement. "Mum says the cookies in Wonderland say 'eat me' on them, but I thought that was a tad bit rude. So I made them more polite."

Evie cocked her head to the side to study the cookie.

"Don't even try to figure it out," Freddie whispered. "The girl lives in la-la land."

"Now, Dino," Ally was saying sternly to the cat, who had just appeared from the kitchen, "I want you to be a good, polite kitty today. Don't eat off anyone's plate. Don't sip anyone's tea, even if it's chamomile, your favorite. Don't insult anyone. And remember to put all your rubbish in the bin."

"See what I mean?" Freddie whispered to Evie. "She thinks the cat can understand her."

"Well, of course he can understand me." Ally had clearly heard the last part. "I'm speaking proper English, aren't I?"

The cat let out a meow and leapt onto the cake table, immediately sticking out his tongue to try to lick the frosting. "No!" Ally cried, shooing him away. "Naughty kitty! Very rude kitty!"

Freddie shot Evie an "I told you so" look. Evie just giggled and placed the cookie in question back on the plate.

The guests, including the rest of the members of the Auradonnas, started to arrive a few minutes later, and by five p.m. the tea shop was packed and the party was in full swing. People were eating cake, drinking tea, dancing to Lonnie's Wonderland-themed music, and buying so many raffle tickets they sold out and Ally had to make more.

Halfway through the party, Freddie grabbed a "please take nourishment from me" cookie and sidled up next to Ally, who was standing in the far corner of the shop, surveying the party.

"So, pretty good, huh?" Freddie asked. "The cards really came through for you, didn't they?"

But then Freddie noticed that Ally didn't look very *happy*. She looked more worried. "Yes, but do you think there might be *too* many people?"

"It's a fund-raiser," Freddie reminded her. "There can never be too many people at a fund-raiser. Just look at all the money you've made for the new costumes."

"I suppose," Ally said, still sounding hesitant. "But people do look a little squished."

Freddie peered into the crowd. She had to admit that Ally had a point. It was getting a little stuffy in there. There were so many bodies crammed inside the tea shop she could barely see the black-and-white checkered rug on the floor anymore. And people were still streaming through the door. In fact, every time someone new entered, the giant mass of bodies seemed to migrate toward Ally and Freddie.

"There are people here that I've never even seen before," Ally said as a group of giggling girls pushed up against them. Ally quickly stepped onto the silk chaise longue next to her to avoid getting trampled.

"Yeah," Freddie said, joining her atop the chair. "I heard people have been driving in from halfway across the kingdom."

From that higher vantage point, Freddie had a much better view of the room. It was pretty crazy in there. There wasn't an inch of available space. People were pressed against the walls and crammed into corners. Even the kitchen was full.

"Maybe we should stop letting people in," Ally suggested.

"Are you kidding?" Freddie replied. "We can't do that! You asked the cards how to get people to your party, and now there are people at your party!"

"Yes, but—"

"And the more people you have," Freddie reminded

her, "the more money you're going to make from the raffle and the better costumes you're going to be able to buy for the finale."

Ally pursed her lips, looking conflicted. "Well, perhaps we should at least move all the furniture into the back. Just to make some more room."

Freddie nodded. "Good idea."

With the help of Mal and Evie, the girls were able to push all the couches, lounges, chairs, and tables through the crowd and into the back room, which was empty apart from a bunch of plumbing pipes and cleaning equipment. It was a tight squeeze, and they had to stack the furniture and shove it against the wall, but they were able to make it all fit.

"Ah," Ally said, letting out a breath when she saw how much more room there was. "Loads better."

A few hours later, after they'd sold more than three hundred raffle tickets, the winner was chosen. It was a girl who'd come all the way from South Riding and had heard about the party from Jordan's Web show.

She chose to ask the mirror which boy she should invite to an upcoming dance at her school. The mirror revealed a handsome brunette with dimples. It was clearly the right choice, because the girl squealed in delight when she saw his face in the glass.

After the last cookie had been consumed and the last cup of tea had been drunk, slowly the tea shop started to empty out until just Ally and Freddie were left.

Ally let out a contented sigh as she finished counting the money in the cash box. "Wow. I can't believe how much we raised! We're going to be able to buy the *best* costumes ever!" She glanced at Freddie, who was licking frosting off her cake fork. "Thank you for helping me, Freddie. You're a good friend."

Friend?

Freddie bristled at the word and nearly choked on her frosting. She peered suspiciously around the tea shop to make sure there were no lingering guests to have heard Ally say that. She refused to get a reputation around there for being friends with AKs.

Freddie swallowed. "I didn't do anything. Thank the cards."

Ally shook her head. "But you were the one who *read* the cards. And you were the one who came with me to Evie's room and helped me convince her to let us use her mirror as a raffle prize. You did a lot!"

Freddie didn't want to remind Ally that she had done

those things so she could get into the Auradonnas. She didn't think that would go over very well. So she just mumbled, "Yeah, well, that's what friends are for." Then she cleared her throat and casually added, "So, then, I guess I'll see you at Auradonnas practice in a few days?"

Dino emerged from under the dessert table and let out a soft meow. Ally smiled and bent down to scoop him into her arms. "Yup. See you at practice!"

Freddie grinned wildly as she headed for the door of the tea shop. She was feeling pretty proud of herself. She'd done exactly what the cards had told her to do: she'd come to the tea shop; she'd granted Ally a favor; and now she was going to get exactly what she wanted.

She was going to be a member of the Auradonnas!

But just before she reached the exit, she suddenly remembered something and spun back around. "One more thing," she said with a serious tone. "You can't tell *anyone* that we used the cards, okay?"

Ally was already off in her own world again, snuggling the cat and whispering nonsense into his ear. "Hmmm?" she asked, barely looking up.

Freddie walked over to Ally and snapped her fingers in front of Ally's face.

"Pay attention. This is important. Unless you want

to get us *both* kicked out of Auradon Prep, you can't tell a single soul about the Shadow Cards."

"Oh," Ally said, scratching the cat between the ears. "Of course. Not a soul."

"Can I trust you?" Freddie asked.

Ally scoffed at the question. "Of course you can trust me. I'm an *AK*. Your secret is safe with me." Then she went back to kissing and cuddling the cat.

But as Freddie left the tea shop, she wasn't feeling as confident as she would have liked. She stepped onto the well-lit pathway that led through campus, her shadow emerging under the overhead streetlamps and following closely beside her.

The whole way back to the dorm, Freddie couldn't help wondering, *How much can you really trust an AK?*

HIGH STAKES

*Ally had better keep her mouth shut, or
we'll both get kicked out of Auradon Prep!*

And things are finally starting to go my way. . . .

The next Auradonna practice wasn't until the next day,
and Freddie was growing more and more restless waiting.
It didn't help that she still had no one to hang out with.

Mal was too busy helping Ben prepare for his Auradon
royal tour, and Evie was too busy sewing the costumes
for the tour's entourage. That meant Freddie spent most
of the day lounging around in her dorm room by herself,
shuffling her Shadow Cards while she rehearsed all the
parts of the Auradonnas' competition songs so she could
be ready for practice.

It was a few hours after dinner the night following

the big fund-raiser tea party when there was a knock on Freddie's door. She was in the middle of an especially difficult harmony part from the Auradonnas' finale song, the one they would sing only if they got into the finals. When she heard the knock, she fell quiet and hid her deck of Shadow Cards under her pillow.

Freddie didn't get many visitors, so she wondered if CJ had sent her another message in a bottle . . . or, better yet, a message in a skull. But when she opened the door, she was shocked to see Jordan standing there.

Again.

"I'm beginning to think you're stalking me," Freddie said, placing a hand on her hip.

Jordan ignored her and eagerly pushed her way into the dorm room, shutting the door behind her. Then she started pacing. And rambling. "I told myself the whole way here, 'Don't do it. Don't get mixed up in that stuff. It's too dangerous. Plus, you're a genie. You have your own powers.' But of course a genie can't make wishes for herself. Ugh!" She pulled on the ends of her pink-striped black hair. "It's that Snow White and her stupid celebrity show. It's not fair. She has more equipment. She has assistants. And a marketing team. I'm just me! How can I possibly compete?"

Freddie stood by the door, gaping at her in confusion.

Why is Jordan pacing and talking nonsense in my dorm room?

"Um . . ." Freddie began, but she was quickly cut off.

"I almost didn't come. I mean, I turned around three times but then I turned back around, because Ally said it was fine. But you know, Ally, she can be a little . . . la-di-da. You know. She gets that from her mother. I mean, the girl followed a white rabbit down a hole. Who does that?"

At the mention of Ally's name, Freddie felt her body tense up as a shiver of dread passed over her. "Jordan," she said warily, "why are you here?"

Jordan finally stopped pacing and turned to face Freddie. There was desperation in her eyes. Freddie recognized it immediately.

Jordan took a huge breath and exhaled loudly. "I need to use your Shadow Cards."

EXPOSED HAND

Do they not know what a
secret is in Auradon?

I thought these AK kids were always bragging
about how honorable they are.

Now it was Freddie's turn to pace and rant. "I knew I should never have trusted Ally! I knew she'd betray me! I can't believe it!"

"Hey," Jordan said, attempting to calm Freddie down, "chill out. I'm not going to tell anyone. I'm an AK, I can be trusted!"

Freddie harrumphed. "Yeah, that's exactly what Ally said."

"Well, to be fair, she only told *me*, and it was only

because she saw how upset I was," Jordan argued. "You see, up until a few hours ago, I had the most popular Web show in Auradon! Then Snow White released footage of Sneezy's son blowing his nose in Auto-Tune, and her numbers skyrocketed! I have to do something! I can't let her supplant me like that!"

"So you want to ask my Shadow Cards how to get more Web show viewers?" Freddie asked in disbelief.

"Yes! Please help me. I'm desperate."

"How do I know *you* won't go off and tell someone else and then, before I know it, the whole school—and Fairy Godmother—knows about my cards?"

"You clearly have never met a genie. We have a code of ethics. I would never do that."

Freddie looked at Jordan, trying to decide whether to believe her. She'd already trusted one AK, and look where that had gotten her.

"Please!" Jordan begged. "I have to take Snow White down!"

Freddie smiled. She liked Jordan. She was about as close to a VK as you could get in Auradon. She decided if there was anyone who deserved to use her Shadow Cards, it was sassy Jordan. And who knew? Maybe after that, she and Jordan could be friends.

Plus—Freddie had to admit—using the cards was fun. She needed a little excitement in her life.

Freddie pulled out the deck from under her pillow. "Now, you *promise* you won't tell anyone?"

Jordan drew an invisible *G* over her chest. "Genie's honor."

"I don't know what that means."

Jordan rolled her eyes. "It means no, I won't tell anyone."

Freddie sighed. "Fine. Come sit down."

She smoothed the comforter and spread the cards out in a straight line. Jordan gently lowered herself onto the bed and stared intensely at the cards. "Huh," she said, sounding disappointed.

"What?"

"Nothing, I just thought they'd be . . . I don't know, scarier or something."

Freddie scoffed. "They're scary."

Jordan shrugged. "*-Ish.*"

Trying to ignore the jab, Freddie took a deep breath and held her hands over the cards. She immediately felt her body hum with energy. Her shadow trembled in anticipation of being released.

"Masters of the Shadow Land, I call upon—"

Jordan snorted, stopping Freddie mid chant.

"What?" Freddie snapped.

"Seriously? Masters of the Shadow Land? That's just a tad bit corny, don't you think?"

Freddie scoffed. "Do you want their help or not?"

Jordan sat up straighter. "Yes. Absolutely. Sorry."

Freddie cleared her throat and restarted the chant. "Masters of the Shadow Land, I call upon your knowing hand. I offer you this sinner's song, to guide the path she walks upon."

Once again, Freddie's shadow morphed into a dark snake of smoke and slithered ominously over the back sides of the cards.

"Now that's more like it!" Jordan said, rubbing her hands together.

The snake coiled and curved until it formed its question mark.

"Go ahead," Freddie said. "Tell the cards what you want."

"Do I have to compliment them first?"

Freddie chuckled. "No, that's just an Ally thing."

Jordan stared at the cards and spoke very clearly. "How do I get more viewers for my Web show so I can put that Snow White chick at number two, where she belongs?"

Freddie stifled a giggle and they both bent forward to watch the purple ball of light bounce from card to card, finally landing on the fourth card from the left, which began to pulse urgently.

Freddie nodded toward it. "There's your answer."

Jordan flipped over the card, revealing a picture of a candlelit hallway that seemed to go on forever. Then the hallway started to move as the card came to life. Freddie felt like she was flying down the hallway, floating just inches above the ground. The picture turned left, through a grand arched doorway, and Freddie instantly recognized the room it had entered.

"It's the banquet hall," Jordan said.

"And look," Freddie said, pointing to the depiction of the familiar long table, filled with pastries, eggs, and fruit. "The table is set for breakfast."

"Why is the card showing me the banquet hall at breakfast?" Jordan asked with a slight turn to her upper lip.

Freddie shrugged. "I don't know."

"You're the shadow . . . whatever . . . person. Aren't *you* supposed to interpret the cards?"

"Why does everyone keep assuming that?" Freddie asked as she bent forward and looked at the picture again. The card was now frozen inside the banquet hall.

"Maybe it's trying to tell you to film your next episode here. During breakfast."

"In the banquet hall?"

"I don't know. You're the Web show . . . whatever . . . person. You figure it out."

Jordan tilted her head. "Hmmm. Well, there *is* really good light in there. And I've always wanted to do an 'Inside the World of Auradon Prep' special. I guess I could give it a try. It can't hurt, right?"

Freddie nodded. "It definitely can't hurt."

"Okay, I'll do it!" With renewed energy, Jordan jumped off the bed and sashayed into the hallway, but not before calling out, "Thanks, Freddie. Ally was right about you. You're pretty cool."

Freddie felt her lips twitching as they fought to break into a smile. She couldn't help feeling a twinge of excitement at the compliment. She kind of liked that Jordan thought she was cool. But she also didn't want to get a reputation for being friends with AKs, so she quickly schooled her face and mumbled, "Yeah, well, don't tell anyone that, okay?"

ALL IN

You know, I kind of liked
helping Jordan and Ally.

Wait, is Auradon Prep making me soft?

The next morning, Freddie woke up to find she had completely slept through breakfast and was late to her History of Auradon class. She bounded out of bed and pulled back the curtains, blinking against the too-bright light that streamed through the windows.

Freddie liked to sleep in complete darkness, because it reminded her of home, but it was hard with all the windows around Auradon Prep. So she'd had to fashion some black curtains to block all the sunlight.

She got dressed in a hurry, barely bothering to do her

hair, and ran out of the dorm toward her classroom. But when she arrived, she found Jordan standing in front of the classroom door, waiting for Freddie with her arms crossed.

"Where have you been?" Jordan demanded. "I've been looking everywhere for you."

She sounded mad. Freddie wondered if something had gone wrong with the Web show and Jordan was going to blame her for it.

So she steeled herself and went on the defensive. "Look, whatever happened with your Web show, I'm not responsible. I have no control over what the cards—"

"What are you talking about?" Jordan interrupted, hands on her hips. "Of course, you're responsible."

Freddie balked slightly. "I mean, yes, I'm the shadow huntress, but that doesn't mean you can blame me for anything."

Jordan cocked an eyebrow. "Shadow huntress? Really? That's what you're going with?"

Freddie huffed. "The title is a work in progress."

"Well, whatever you are, you're not getting out of this. I know you VKs don't like to get compliments or whatever, but you deserve just as much credit for this success as I do."

Freddie opened her mouth to argue before realizing what Jordan had just said.

Wait a minute. Success?

"What?" Freddie asked.

Jordan's eyes lit up. "The episode! It's a *huge* hit. You haven't seen it yet?"

Freddie shook her head, and Jordan whipped out her phone and turned it around so Freddie could see the screen. "I uploaded it right after breakfast and it's already gone viral."

Jordan pressed play and Freddie's eyes were glued to the screen as she watched Ben—*King* Ben—eating what looked like a bowl of porridge without using his hands. The white gooey breakfast was all over him—on his face, down the front of his shirt, even in his hair.

"What is this?" Freddie asked with a chuckle.

Jordan beamed with pride. "So, I was going to just shoot some footage around the banquet hall—you know, like Auradon Prep kids studying before class, and eating pastries, or whatever. But then Ben and Chad got into this hilarious porridge-eating contest. They challenged each other to see who could finish their bowl first without using any hands." Jordan let out a hoot of laughter. "Everyone in Auradon is loving it! It's a celebrity exclusive! I'm almost at a million views and it's been up less than an hour. And look at all these comments!"

Jordan swiped up on the screen, and Freddie read some of the things people had written about the video.

He's definitely his father's son!
Hilarious! #BeastJunior
King vs Food. Awesome!!!

"Isn't it great?" Jordan asked. But before Freddie could answer, Jordan turned the screen back toward her and hit refresh. "Another hundred new subscribers! Your cards are *genius*. They must have somehow known this was going to happen." Jordan seemed to notice something on her phone and her smile fell. "Oh, no. We're late. We'd better get to class. But we have to hang out later so we can talk more about this. Okay?"

Freddie nodded. "For sure."

As she followed Jordan into their history classroom, Freddie felt a swell of pride rise inside her. Her Shadow Cards had done it *again*. Not only had they gotten her a spot in the Auradonnas *and* rescued Ally's party *and* saved Jordan's Web show, now it seemed they might have solved her little loneliness problem, too.

WINNING HAND

Wow. Those cards really are magic.

And I know how to use them like a pro.

By the time the last class of the day let out, *everyone* was talking about Jordan's Web show. It had gotten over two million views since Jordan had posted it that morning. At lunch, Freddie even saw a table full of students attempting to impersonate Ben's porridge fiasco with their bowls of soup. And every time she saw Jordan around school, someone was congratulating her on her brilliant episode.

Freddie was feeling proud of herself. Not only for what she'd done for Jordan, but obviously also for what she'd done for herself. Her first Auradonnas practice was in less than two hours!

Ally still hadn't told the group about their new

member. She insisted they wait until Freddie's first rehearsal, claiming it would be better to announce it to the group while Freddie was there and could show off her singing chops.

As she walked back to the dorm from her Remedial Goodness 101 class, Freddie slipped her hand into her pocket and ran her thumb affectionately over the deck, like she was saying thank you.

She couldn't believe she was actually going to be singing with the number one a cappella group in all of Auradon! She was one step closer to her big dream of becoming a famous jazz singer. She could already feel the bright lights shining down on her on that stage. She could already hear the roar of the crowd. She could already—

BAM!

Freddie must not have been watching where she was going, because she tripped over a tree root and landed on the grass with an *"ooph!"*

"Oh, dear," someone said with a cheerful voice. "Are you all right?"

Freddie peered up to see Headmistress Fairy Godmother standing over her.

"Yes, I'm fine." Freddie nervously jumped to her feet and slipped her hand into her dress pocket to check for the cards.

But the cards weren't there.

Panicked, Freddie glanced around her, spotting the deck right next to Fairy Godmother's feet!

Her heart started to race. If Fairy Godmother saw those cards, everything would be ruined! She'd confiscate them for sure and probably kick Freddie out of school! Then Freddie would never get to sing in the Auradonnas!

She needed to distract Fairy Godmother with something so she could bend down and scoop up the cards without her noticing.

What I wouldn't give for a sidekick right now, Freddie thought, missing CJ more than ever. CJ would know what to do. She'd run into Fairy Godmother. Or pull the fire alarm. Or make a loud—

CRASH!

Freddie and Fairy Godmother both looked over to see Carlos's dog, Dude, running wild through the campus with Carlos chasing him. Dude had just knocked over a table of supplies that the nature club had been setting up.

Freddie moved quickly, using the distraction to bend down, scoop up her cards, and return them to her pocket.

"Carlos!" Fairy Godmother said, turning to join the

chase. "I told you to keep that dog on a leash!"

Freddie breathed out a sigh of relief and continued toward the dorm. But just before she walked through the front door, she felt someone's hand on her arm.

"I need to talk to you," he said.

She turned to see it was Carlos. He was completely out of breath, but he had Dude clutched under one arm.

"Okay," Freddie said. "So talk."

Carlos's eyes darted back and forth suspiciously, like he was afraid of being followed by spies.

"Not here. Come with me." He led Freddie away from the dorm, across the tourney field, and into a small shed that was filled with uniforms and tourney sticks. He placed Dude on the ground, and the dog started to sniff around.

"What is this place?" Freddie asked.

"It's the tourney shed. Look, Jordan told me what you did for her."

Freddie felt her stomach swoop. *"What?"*

"She told me you helped her. With your Shadow Cards. Dude! I didn't even know you'd brought them with you."

Dude perked up his head at his name. Carlos laughed. "Not you Dude. Her dude."

Dude's head tilted in confusion.

"Never mind," Carlos muttered.

Freddie's teeth instinctively clenched. "Jordan! I swear those AK kids *cannot* keep a secret."

Carlos laughed. "I could have told you that. Anyway, I need your help, too."

Freddie narrowed her eyes. "Why should I help you?"

"Who do you think let Dude loose back there?"

Freddie thought about the giant crash that had saved her from getting in trouble just a moment earlier. "You did that on purpose?"

"Yeah," Carlos said. "I saw you drop the cards. I helped you. So now you owe me, right?"

Freddie sighed. He was right. She *did* owe him. "What's your problem?"

Carlos bit his lip, looking embarrassed. "The truth is I'm tired of Jay getting all the attention on the tourney field. I mean, he's a superstar and I'm just the short shrimpy VK who gets knocked around a lot."

Freddie suppressed a giggle. The last tourney game she'd watched had been exactly as Carlos just described. Jay had scored all the goals and Carlos had spent most of the time on the ground.

"So you want the Shadow Cards to make you a better tourney player?" Freddie confirmed. "I mean, the cards are good, but they're not *that* good."

Carlos scoffed and gave her a friendly punch in the arm. "Ha-ha. Very funny. I don't know what I want. We have a game in less than an hour and I just need some help. I need to get noticed out there. I'm sick of being trampled by everyone . . . even my own teammates."

Freddie sighed and removed the cards from the pocket of her dress. "Fine. Let's get this over with."

She sat down on the floor of the tourney shed next to Dude and fanned the cards out in front of her.

Carlos smiled, looking extremely relieved, and sat down across from Freddie. "Thanks, Freddie. This is really wicked of you."

Freddie shrugged. "What can I say? I'm feeling pretty wicked today. Okay, let's do this." She extended her hand and let it float just above the cards. Then she recited the spell.

"Masters of the Shadow Land, I call upon your knowing hand. I offer you this sinner's song, to guide the path he walks upon."

The cards immediately responded, and her shadow morphed into the misty black snake that formed a question mark.

"Go ahead," Freddie said. "Ask for what you want."

Carlos cleared his throat and spoke to the cards. "How do I become a tourney star?"

The answer came swiftly. The dancing ball of light landed on a card right in front of Carlos. He flipped it over and they both leaned in to see what the card had to say.

It was a picture of a tourney field. It was empty. But then, a second later, the picture came to life and a team stormed the field.

"Hey," Carlos said. "That's the Sherwood Forest Falcons. We're playing them today."

They watched the Falcons run around the field. When one of the Falcons' forwards had possession of the tourney ball, the entire team ran into the kill zone and converged in the same spot, forming a protective circle around the forward with the ball.

"What are they doing?" Carlos asked, his furry eyebrows pinching together as he watched.

Then, in the chaos of the dragon fire coming from the cannons on the sidelines, one Falcon snuck away from the huddle and started walking slowly toward the goal, like he was just repositioning himself. Both Freddie and Carlos had to lean in close and squint to notice that he had the tourney ball. But no one on the field seemed to notice. They were too distracted by the strange huddle that was happening in the kill zone.

"Whoa," Carlos said. "I've never seen anyone do

that. Do you see how slow he's walking so he doesn't attract any attention? That's really sneaky!"

The image on the card kept moving until the forward who had snuck away with the ball made a goal and the Falcon cheerleaders went crazy.

Freddie let out a gasp. "I think the cards are showing you the Falcon's big play for today's game!"

Carlos looked up and met her gaze with excitement. "You're right! And now that I know what it is, I can intercept it and save the game!"

Freddie smiled a delicious villainous grin. "All hail Carlos De Vil, the new tourney star."

RAISE THE STAKES

I got the AKs what they wanted. Now it's time for me to get what I want.

Watch me enchant these folks at the Auradonnas rehearsal.

As she watched Carlos stroll onto the field to warm up for his big tourney game, Freddie gave herself a mental pat on the back. She was getting pretty good at this saving-the-day stuff. Unfortunately, she wouldn't be able to stick around to watch the game, because her Auradonnas practice was at the same time.

Freddie turned and headed back toward the dorm. The sun was high in the sky, making Freddie's shadow look squat, like a hunched-over old lady with a cane.

"Good work today," she said, commending the shadow. "You're on a roll!"

When Freddie reached the dorm, she hurried up the steps to her room. She wanted to get in some last-minute rehearsals before the *actual* rehearsal. Even though Ally had promised her a spot in the group, she still had to impress the rest of the singers. She still had to prove she *deserved* that spot. She didn't want to make a fool of herself during her very first rehearsal—especially when their big national competition was coming up in only a few days.

But when she burst through her door, she was startled to find Jordan in her room, sitting on her bed.

For a second, Freddie wondered if she'd barged into the wrong room. But then she saw CJ's makeshift pirate ship sail on the other bed and knew that she was in the right place.

"What are you doing in my room?" Freddie asked accusingly.

Jordan stood up from the bed and stomped over to Freddie, a deep scowl on her face. "You tricked me," she snarled.

Jordan sounded angry. But Freddie wasn't going to be fooled by that again.

Freddie laughed. "Is this a thing you do? Where you pretend to be mad but you're actually ecstatic?"

Jordan looked confused. "What? No! I *am* mad. I never should have trusted you. You're evil. You and your shadow! Pure evil."

Freddie smiled. "Thank you."

"That's not a compliment."

"It is where I come from."

Jordan narrowed her eyes and glared at Freddie. "I can't believe I let you manipulate me like that. I should have known never to trust the daughter of the shadow man, the most deceitful villain to ever live."

Freddie touched her chest. "Again, thank you."

"Stop thanking me!" Jordan yelled. "You ruined my life!"

"Wait, what now?" Freddie asked. "I thought I *saved* your life. Did you forget already? Web show? Big hit? Millions of views? Ring a bell?"

"My Web show is *over*!" Jordan cried. "And it's all your fault!"

Freddie's eyebrows knit together. "Okay, I think I missed something."

"Look!" Jordan said, shoving her phone in Freddie's face. Freddie blinked in confusion as she attempted to read an *Auradonian Times* news article that was on the screen.

But she didn't have to read it. The headline told her all she needed to know.

KING BEN'S ROYAL TOUR DELAYED INDEFINITELY

"Delayed?" Freddie said, her questioning eyes darting back to Jordan.

Jordan lowered the phone. "Yes! Because of *my* Web show! The episode of him gobbling porridge like a beast went viral. Everyone at Auradon Prep loves it, but his advisors worry that no one can take him seriously as king right now. They've postponed the entire tour until this blows over."

Freddie cringed. "Ouch. Mal's gonna be mad."

"*I'm* mad!" Jordan said, pointing at herself. "Me. This is about *me*. I'm the victim here."

"You?"

She huffed. "After Fairy Godmother found out it was *my* Web show that aired the exclusive, she prohibited me from filming another episode for a month! Do you know what happens to Web shows that don't post for an entire month? Everyone forgets about them. They die a slow, painful death."

"Sounds fun," Freddie said.

"Stop making jokes! This. Is. Your. Fault."

"Whoa, whoa," Freddie said soothingly. "Let's just calm down and be rational about this. I'm sure we can—"

"There's nothing to be rational about!" Jordan yelled. "You knew this would happen. You tricked me into using those cards."

Now Freddie was getting mad. "Hold up. I did *not* know this would happen."

"Why should I believe you? You're a VK, and VKs lie all the time."

"Well, that's true," Freddie admitted, "but I'm not lying now. I swear. Look, let's go over to Mad for Tea, have a scone, and talk about this calmly. I'm sure we can figure out how to fix this."

Jordan's mouth twitched as she thought about whether to listen to Freddie. "Fine," she said, stalking toward the door. "But you'd better fix this. Or I'm telling Fairy Godmother the truth. The *whole* truth."

Freddie cringed. Fairy Godmother could *not* know that Freddie had used shadow magic at Auradon Prep. She'd be expelled.

Plus, Auradonnas practice started in an hour, which meant she had sixty minutes to convince Jordan not to turn her in *and* get herself across campus to the chapel.

She would have to rock some serious velvet voice to pull that off.

But a few minutes later, when they arrived at Mad for Tea, Freddie felt her hopes crash and her heart sink to the bottom of her chest

Uh-oh, she thought as they stepped inside the tea shop. *This might be more complicated than I thought.*

Freddie glanced down at her feet. But she couldn't even *see* her feet.

Because she and Jordan were standing in ankle-deep water.

FOUL HAND

Uh-oh. Maybe I'm not the shadow sorceress after all.

"You!" Ally cried as soon as she and Jordan entered the Mad for Tea shop. "You horrible, terrible, evil villain, you!"

Freddie smiled. "Is this Compliment Your Fellow Student Day or something?"

"What happened here?" Jordan asked, lifting up her now soaked boot.

Ally started crying. "It was the furniture! When we pushed it into the back room during the party, one of the chairs shoved up against a water pipe. The pressure was too much! The pipe burst this morning and flooded the whole tea shop! The plumber told me how much it's going to cost just to fix the broken pipe and it's *all* the money we made from the fund-raiser! And that doesn't even include getting all this water out—which means we won't have anything left over to buy the new costumes. And my mum is coming home from her vacation in two days and she's going to see this disaster and I'm going to get in trouble. And it's all *her* fault." Ally jabbed her finger at Freddie.

"Hold on. Back up," Freddie said, putting up her hands in a defensive gesture. "Why is everyone around here suddenly blaming *me* for their problems? I didn't do this."

"The whole reason this happened was because of *your* stupid Shadow Cards!" Ally cried. "They told me to go to Evie's room so I would get the idea for the raffle prize. And it was because of that raffle prize that we had too many people in the tea shop and had to move all the furniture to make room!"

"Hey, those cards got you exactly what you wanted. You wanted people to come to your party. If we hadn't used the cards—"

Ally cut her off. "If we hadn't used the cards, none of this would have happened. I told you the party was getting too big. People were showing up from halfway across the kingdom to get a chance to use the mirror! If we had just hung fliers around school like I suggested, we would have had a successful *normal*-sized party and the pipe never would have broken."

Freddie pondered that for a moment. She glanced around the tea shop for her shadow and found it on the wall behind her.

Is that true? she asked the shadow silently in her mind. *Did the cards really cause this?*

"You're the one who convinced me to use the cards in the first place!" Ally went on. "You said it would be the best way to get people to the party." She gestured wildly to the flooded tea shop. "And now look what kind of trouble I'm in! And it's all your fault!"

"Okay, I think that's a bit of a stretch," Freddie said.

"Actually," Jordan said pensively, "she has a point."

"No, she doesn't," Freddie fired back.

"If *I* hadn't used the cards," Jordan went on, tapping her finger against her chin, "then I never would have gone to the banquet hall to film my Web show episode. I never would have caught King Ben on camera eating porridge like an animal. It never would have gone viral. The royal tour never would have been put on hold. And Fairy Godmother never would have prohibited me from filming my Web show!" She finished that last part with the excitement of a sleuth who had just solved the crime of the century.

"Exactly!" Ally said, pointing at Freddie. "Those cards are evil!"

"Now, just hold on a minute," Freddie said. "Do you hear how ridiculous you both sound right now? Are you really going to blame a pack of *cards* for what happened to you?"

"YES!" Ally and Jordan said at once.

"That seems a little unfair."

Just then, Jordan's and Ally's phones beeped at the same time. Jordan looked at her screen and her scowl deepened. She turned the phone around to show Freddie the message.

Evie: Oh my gosh! Carlos just tried to block some crazy play during the tourney game and dislocated his shoulder! We won but the doctor says he probably can't play for three more games!

"Let me guess," Jordan said in a snarky voice. "You used the cards on Carlos, too?"

Freddie opened her mouth to speak but no sound came out.

Carlos got injured blocking that play?

She was starting to worry that Ally and Jordan might be on to something. What if the cards were really

98

at fault for all this? What if the shadow spirits that lived inside them had purposefully done this? What if the cards really were evil?

Well, of course, they're evil, Freddie reasoned. *But I got what I wanted out of them, didn't I?*

Or had she? Freddie soon realized that Ally hadn't yet talked to the group about letting her in. She was supposed to do that at practice, which started in half an hour.

Freddie fidgeted nervously with the hem of her dress, trying to figure out what to do. She needed to find a way to smooth everything over.

"C'mon, Ally," Freddie said in her charming velvet voice. "Let's talk through this on the way to the chapel, okay? We're going to be late for practice."

"Practice?" Ally yelled. "There is no practice!"

Freddie felt her stomach tense. "What do you mean, there's no practice?"

"I canceled it. I have to deal with this mess!" She kicked her foot, splashing a bunch of water toward Freddie and Jordan. Jordan jumped out of the way. Freddie was not as quick, and the water splashed in her face.

Freddie tried to remain calm, but it was getting more and more difficult. She gritted her teeth to keep from losing her temper. "But today was the day you were going to tell the Auradonnas I was joining the group."

Ally looked at Jordan in disbelief and then back to Freddie. "You really expect me to get you into the group after what you did?"

"A deal's a deal," Freddie reminded her.

"This wasn't a deal!" Ally screeched. "You tricked us. Both of us. And poor Carlos. We should have seen it coming. Your father is Dr. Facilier, after all. Of course, we shouldn't have trusted you. What were we thinking?"

"You can't go back on your word," Freddie said, getting angry.

"Why not?" Ally cried, tears streaming down her face. "You VKs go back on your word all the time."

"You're the ones who couldn't keep a secret about the cards after you promised you would!" Freddie angrily reminded them.

"Hey!" Jordan said. "Ally was the one who told me."

Ally reeled on Jordan. "And you told Carlos!"

"Not the same thing," Jordan said defensively. "I told a VK. You told an AK."

"What does that matter?" Ally retorted.

"I think it matters," Jordan reasoned.

"Well, I only told *you* because I thought I could trust you," Ally said. "But apparently you're just as bad as the VKs."

Jordan scoffed. "Speak for yourself!"

"I would never speak for you," Ally said to Jordan with disgust.

"Good!" Jordan screamed. "Because I'd hate for everyone to think *my* head was in the clouds, too!"

And soon all three of them were yelling and pointing fingers at one another.

"Enough!" Ally finally screeched at the top of her lungs, causing everyone to fall silent. She turned her angry, tear-filled eyes to Freddie and in a slightly calmer voice said, "You know, maybe if you had just helped me spread the word about the party—maybe if you had just been *nice* to me, instead of tricking me with dark shadow magic—I would have let you into the group."

"I didn't know this would happen!" Freddie insisted.

"I don't believe you," Ally said, "because I don't trust you. And that's why I'll *never* let you into the Auradonnas." Ally turned and sloshed into the kitchen.

"Well," Jordan said brusquely. "I guess that's *one* thing Ally and I agree on. I don't trust you, either." Then she turned and trudged out the front door, leaving Freddie alone with her shadow in ankle-deep water, listening to the tiny ripples that lapped against the walls of the flooded tea shop.

FOLD 'EM?

Shadow Cards? More like shady cards!

I'm further away from singing with the Auradonnas than ever.

Freddie couldn't sleep that night. She tossed and turned, thinking about everything that had happened. She didn't understand how so much could fall apart so fast.

That afternoon everything had been great. Freddie was going to join the Auradonnas, Ally had raised enough money to buy new costumes, Jordan had the most popular Web show in all of Auradon, and Carlos was going to be a tourney star. The cards had given all of them exactly what they'd wanted.

And now, after only a few hours, it seemed like the cards had taken it all away.

The tea shop was ruined and the money for the

costumes had to go to fix the broken pipe.

Jordan couldn't film any episodes of her Web show for a month.

Carlos was in the infirmary with a busted shoulder.

And what about me? Freddie thought as she lay in the pitch darkness of her dorm room. *I lost my only shot at getting into the Auradonnas. The only thing that made me want to stay at Auradon Prep is gone.*

It was like they had all paid a price for using the cards to get what they wanted.

Freddie suddenly remembered a conversation she'd had with her dad when she was a little girl.

"Why do they call you the shadow man?" she'd asked him once as he tucked her into bed. The small candle by her bedside was casting a giant, eerie shadow of her father on the wall.

Her father smiled his dark, sinister smile and said, "Because I demand a price for everything I do. Because every favor I grant has a shadow side, a dark consequence. That's how you become powerful. That's how you *win*."

Then he'd blown out the candle, extinguishing his dark shadow, and left the room.

Now Freddie sat up in her bed and turned on the light, causing shadows to appear all around her Auradon Prep dorm room. The low light made them all twisted and disfigured. The four posts of her bed looked like long, sharp fingernails. The dresser with the mirror on top looked like an ugly monster with horns. The make-shift pirate ship sail that CJ had fashioned on her own bed looked like a murky swamp.

And then there was Freddie's own shadow, sitting faithfully beside her on the bed. It appeared to be mocking her.

"I thought you were my friend," she whispered quietly to the shadow. She could almost hear it laughing in response, calling her a fool. Because that's exactly what she felt like: a fool. She had trusted the cards, she had trusted her own shadow, and both had betrayed her. In a sudden fit of rage, Freddie jumped out of bed and ripped all the sheets off the mattress. But her shadow just slunk to the floor.

She turned on another light, trying to chase it away, but the shadow just jumped across the room to CJ's bed.

Freddie lunged at it, but it was too quick. That shadow was always one step ahead of her, always just managing to elude her. She took a step toward it but it leapt onto the pirate ship sail strung across CJ's bed.

With a roar, Freddie yanked the sail down and threw it to the floor. The shadow settled comfortably in a corner and just watched her.

Fuming and breathless, Freddie stared it down.

"I know how to get rid of you," she threatened.

The shadow didn't reply.

Freddie marched over to the first lamp and switched it off. Her shadow moved obediently closer to her. She swore it looked scared now.

She crept over to the other lamp, the only light left in the room, poised her finger on the cord, and, with an evil grin, pulled down hard.

The dorm room plunged into darkness and her shadow was finally, *finally* gone.

As Freddie stood in the pitch-blackness, breathing heavily, something dawned on her. She switched the light back on and watched all the shadows in the room reappear, including her own.

Every light casts a shadow, she realized.

Everything has a dark side.

Even in Auradon.

"Of course," she whispered aloud. "*Shadow* Cards."

That's why they were called what they were called.

It was just as her father had told her all those years ago.

Every wish has a shadow side.

Every favor has a price.

And now the cards had collected their payment.

BAD DEAL

Have you ever realized your amazing plan
for getting exactly what you wanted had a
dark side you never could have imagined?

Yeah, me too.

Freddie awoke the next morning to find the disaster she
had made of her dorm room, and all the horrors of the
day before came flooding back to her.

The cards had tricked her.

They had promised her things without warning her
of the price.

And worst of all, she worried they weren't finished
collecting.

What if they weren't satisfied with the payments they

had received? What if they wreaked even more havoc on the school? What if she had unknowingly released evil shadow spirits at Auradon Prep and they never *ever* stopped destroying things?

If she had learned anything growing up with her father it was that you should never trust a shadow man. He was always one step ahead of you. He was always finding a way to manipulate the situation. He always wanted more. And that deck of cards was basically just another shadow man.

But that was all in the past. Now she just knew she had to fix this. She had to figure out how to reverse what she'd done to Ally, Jordan, Carlos, and herself. *And* she had to stop the cards from doing any more damage.

The problem was she had no idea how she was going to accomplish that.

When breakfast time rolled around, Freddie didn't even bother going downstairs to the banquet hall. She didn't want to face Ally and Jordan again and she wasn't hungry anyway. There was a sickly, sour feeling in her stomach that she couldn't identify, but it felt like it was eating her alive.

And worst of all, she had no one to talk to about any of it.

Mal was busy consoling Ben about the royal tour Freddie's cards had sabotaged. Evie was busy helping Carlos with his dislocated shoulder (also the fault of the cards). And Jordan and Ally weren't even speaking to her.

It wasn't like Freddie had anyone else to go to. Who around here would even understand? Who at Auradon Prep could possibly know what it's like to deal with evil shadow forces set on ruining your life?

No one there could understand the kind of dark, sinister magic Freddie was dealing with, let alone help.

She simply had to accept the fact that there was no fix to the Shadow Cards. There was no light for this darkness. She couldn't just *undo* a flood in the tea shop or *un*suspend Jordan's Web show or *un*dislocate Carlos's shoulder.

If she was to fix this mess, she'd need to find someone who knew how to counteract shadow magic. Someone with the power to reverse black magic spells. And the only person she'd ever heard of who could do that was . . .

"Slithering snakes!" Freddie jumped to her feet as an idea came to her. "Why didn't I think of that before?"

She didn't waste another minute; she didn't have another minute to waste. She sprinted out of her dorm room and ran all the way to the banquet hall. She scanned the crowded room until she found Ally and Jordan. They were sitting at separate tables, still not talking to each other after the big fight they'd all gotten into the day before.

They both looked horrible. Ally had puffy eyes, probably from crying all night, and even Jordan, who was always so put together, looked like she'd barely even glanced in a mirror that morning.

Freddie darted over to Ally's table, grabbed her by the hand, yanked her out of her chair, and dragged her toward the other side of the hall. Ally griped and complained the whole way.

"I have to talk to you guys," Freddie said urgently when she and Ally had reached Jordan's table. The two girls would barely even look at each other.

"What?" Jordan asked coldly, glaring at Freddie.

Freddie took a deep breath. "I think I know how to fix this. *All* of this."

Ally looked curious. But it was Jordan who smirked, crossed her arms over her chest, and said, "I'm listening."

Freddie smiled. "How do you guys feel about taking a little field trip the Bayou D'Orleans?"

DEALER'S CHOICE

I have an idea.

I just hope it works!

"What's in the bayou?" Jordan asked once they had all reconvened inside Jordan's lamp, which was basically just her bedroom except it was inside a genie's lamp.

Freddie hadn't wanted to talk about her plan in the middle of the banquet hall because she was afraid someone would overhear.

Freddie's eyes lit up as she prepared to tell Ally and Jordan her big idea. "Someone who can help us undo the Shadow Cards' curse."

Ally looked skeptical. "Who?"

"Mama Odie!" Freddie said with excitement.

"*Who?*" Jordan echoed.

Freddie had expected a better response than that. She sighed. "She's the voodoo queen of the bayou."

"Nuh-uh," Ally immediately retorted. "No more voodoo magic."

"No, you don't understand," Freddie tried to explain. "She uses voodoo for *good*. My dad always hated her. He complained about her constantly. Back when they both lived in the bayou they were rivals. She was the light side and he was the dark side of the voodoo arts. My dad got banished to the Isle of the Lost, but she's still in the bayou! Because she's *good*. She can help us. She can reverse the spell."

"Really?" Jordan asked, and Freddie could tell she was starting to come around.

"Yes, really," Freddie insisted. "She can get you your Web show back and—" she turned to Ally. "She can fix up the tea shop. She'll solve everything!"

"How do you know?" Ally said. "Have you talked to her?"

Freddie balked slightly at this. "No. Not really. But I just know. Dad was always griping about her undoing his best shadow spells. I know if we go see her and tell her what happened, she'll help."

Ally bit her lip. "I don't know. Magic got us into this mess. Is it really the best idea to use it to get out?"

"Well, I'm down," Jordan said.

Ally and Freddie turned toward her and said in unison, "You are?"

"Yeah," Jordan said. "Let's do this. Let's get this show on the road. I need that Web show back ASAP before I start losing subscribers."

Freddie beamed. She knew she liked Jordan.

"B-b-but," Ally stammered, clearly not convinced yet. "But we can't just *leave*."

"The bayou is not that far," Jordan pointed out. "We'll be gone less than a day. I'm in." Jordan made an ambiguous gesture toward Ally. "I don't know about *her*."

"Um," Ally said hesitantly. "Um."

"C'mon," Jordan coaxed with annoyance. "Stop daydreaming for one second and make a decision already!"

"Fine!" Ally yelled. "I'll go." She reeled on Freddie. "But even if this works, I'm still not letting you into the Auradonnas."

"Good," Jordan said, taking command. "Then it's settled. I'll secure the transportation and we'll meet at the King Beast statue in an hour."

An hour later, Freddie showed up at the big statue of King Beast in front of the school.

Ally and Jordan were already there, backs turned toward each other, staring at their phones like they were each pretending the other didn't exist.

Seeing them ignore each other gave Freddie that unfamiliar sickly feeling in her stomach again, the same one she'd had in her dorm room earlier.

What is *that?* she thought. *Whatever it is, I don't like it.*

Freddie cleared her throat. "So, who's ready for an epic adventure into the bayou?" She was trying to sound upbeat in hopes of lifting the girls' spirits. It didn't work. They glanced up at her momentarily, each mumbling something incomprehensible, before returning to their phones. Freddie didn't blame them. She wasn't exactly an *upbeat* kind of girl. Dark and brooding always seemed to fit her best.

She sighed and glanced around the empty street in front of them. "Where's this transportation you were going to secure?" she asked Jordan.

But before Jordan could answer, Freddie heard an obnoxiously shrill honking sound, and a second later, a car in the brightest shade of orange Freddie had *ever* seen pulled up to the curb.

It was a minivan. And Fairy Godmother was driving it.

"Yoo-hoo!" she called out the open window. "Who's ready for a road trip?"

Freddie leaned in to Jordan and whispered. "You've got to be kidding me."

"Is she coming with us?" Ally asked, blinking her huge eyes in wonderment.

"No," Jordan said behind her hand. "I told her we needed transpo for a school project and she offered to let us take her car."

Fairy Godmother opened the car door and hopped out, clasping her hands together. "I just love seeing you three girls working together and getting along so well."

"Say what now?" Freddie asked Jordan.

"Oh, right," Jordan added quietly. "And she thinks we're all the bestest of besties, so just go with it, okay?"

Before either Freddie or Ally could argue, Jordan stretched her arms out wide and pulled both girls into a hug. "I know, right?" she crooned to Fairy Godmother. "I just *love* these two to pieces!"

"I did *not* agree to this," Freddie mumbled under her breath.

"Just play along," Jordan mumbled back as she released them.

Freddie sighed and slipped into her role. "What can I say? These two are the greatest!"

Jordan turned on the charm for Fairy Godmother. "It's so nice of you to let us drive this"—Jordan gestured toward the car—"lovely automobile."

Fairy Godmother glanced back at her minivan and gave a wistful sigh. "It is lovely, isn't it? The color is custom! Pumpkin orange! And it has eighteen cup holders! I call it the Bobbidi Buggy!"

"Well, it's perfect," Jordan said, giving Freddie a nudge.

"Wicked awesome," Freddie added with a totally fake smile.

Fairy Godmother beamed as she handed Jordan the keys.

"Well, you three have fun together!" Fairy Godmother said.

Ally linked arms with Freddie. "I can't imagine us having anything else!" she said in an over-the-top bubbly voice.

"Wonderful!" Fairy Godmother said as she turned and pranced into the castle. As soon as she was out of sight, Ally dropped Freddie's arm, Freddie's smile fell from her face, and Jordan snapped in a brusque tone, "Everybody in. Let's get this over with."

DEAL US IN

So, I'm not 100 percent sure how we'll find Mama Odie. I guess we'll figure that out once this car comes to a halt. And I really hope it does.

I'm starting to wish we had taken that magic carpet.

The car ride to the bayou was uncomfortable, to say the least. No one spoke. Freddie tried to hum a song to pass the time but she was quickly shushed by Ally and Jordan, who apparently wanted to ride in complete silence.

As they drove, Freddie stared out the window and thought about the last time she had visited the bayou with her *real* bestie, CJ.

She wondered what CJ was doing right then. Where she was, who she was meeting. What she was plundering.

It made her smile to think about CJ wreaking havoc on the seas of Auradon in her mighty pirate ship.

Then she wondered what CJ would have done in this situation. Would she have gone out of her way to help a bunch of AKs solve their problems? Even if *she* was the one to blame for them?

Freddie almost laughed aloud at the thought.

Most definitely *not*.

CJ would have just taken off, leaving the mess behind her, the way she always did. She loved leaving disaster in her wake.

But Freddie was different. She realized that now. She didn't want to be *just* a VK. And she certainly didn't want to be an AK, either. She wanted to be something in between.

She wanted to do the right thing.

And she was positive this was it.

Well, *almost* positive.

When they arrived at the bayou, everyone was still grumpy and on edge. Freddie decided to take command of the situation. The faster she could get them all to Mama Odie's and fix this mess, the faster they could put it all behind them.

"Okay," Freddie said, stepping out of the car and

stretching her legs. "We need to figure out a plan."

"A plan?" Ally said, slamming her door. "I thought you said you *had* a plan."

"I do," Freddie said. "My plan is to get to the bayou and find Mama Odie. Now we just need a plan on how to do that."

"You mean, we came all the way out here and you don't even know *where* Mama Odie is?" Jordan shrieked.

"Of course, I know where she is," Freddie defended. "She's *in* the bayou."

Exasperated, Jordan gestured around at the large and bustling city they were currently smack dab in the middle of. "Uh, hello? The bayou is *huge!*"

"This was a terrible idea," Ally cried. "I don't know how I let you two talk me into this. This is going to be a catastrophe. We're never going to find her. The tea shop will never get fixed. And Mum is going to yell at me when she gets home. And . . ."

As Ally continued to rant incessantly, Jordan whispered to Freddie, "She gets a little cranky when she's hungry."

Ally stopped talking and looked eagerly at Jordan. "Hungry? Who's hungry? *You're* hungry? I'm hungry, too. Is anyone else hungry?"

Freddie snorted out a laugh. "Okay, let's get

something to eat and we'll talk about what we're going to do next." Her eyes scanned their surroundings until she spotted the marina in the distance and a familiar little restaurant with a red sign.

Her lips curved into a smile. "C'mon. I know just the place."

The three girls sat at a table in the Bass Notes and Beignets jazz club, stuffing their faces with delicious hot beignets. Freddie could already feel that with sugar in their stomachs and sultry jazz music in their ears, the girls' spirits were lifting.

Freddie was so happy to be back there. It was the most at home she'd felt in a long time.

"I've never heard this kind of music before," Ally said, swaying gently to the beat of the instrumental song coming from the small stage in the back of the club. "What is it?"

Freddie's forehead wrinkled. "You've never heard jazz music before?"

Ally shrugged. "Mum always played classical in the house when I was growing up."

"Well, this is the sound I grew up on," Freddie said.

"It's very . . ." Ally searched for the right word. "Unique."

"Jazz music is super versatile," Freddie explained. "You can pretty much take *any* song and make it jazz."

"Any song?" Ally asked doubtfully.

Freddie nodded and dusted powdered sugar off her hands. "Yeah. Take your Auradonnas final competition song, 'Would You Rather.' If you changed up the percussion a little, slowed it down, added a few extra notes to the harmony, and altered the rhythm, it would sound something like this." Freddie cleared her throat and began to sing the Auradonnas' upbeat, bubbly competition song with a slower, groovier jazz feel.

"Good, bad, dark, light. What you rather be tonight?"

She closed her eyes, feeling the music move through her, letting it overtake her. In fact, she got so lost in the music she didn't even realize that the entire club—including the musicians on the stage—had fallen quiet. . . .

Until she opened her eyes and noticed everyone in the restaurant watching her.

Embarrassed, Freddie quickly finished up her song and the whole room broke into applause. Even Ally and Jordan clapped.

"That was amazing!" Ally said, beaming. Then, as though she suddenly remembered why they were there in the first place, she wiped the grin from her face and added, "I mean, it was all right."

Freddie looked sheepishly around the club and gave a little wave.

A moment later, one of the musicians—a tall, broad-shouldered sax player—stepped down from the stage and approached Freddie. "Dang, girl, you got some vocals on you."

Freddie couldn't help smiling at his familiar southern drawl. "Thank you."

"What brought you into our little club?" he asked.

"We're looking for Mama Odie!" Ally said excitedly. "Do you know where she lives?"

"Sure, I do," the man said. "Everyone round here knows where Mama Odie lives. She's out in a houseboat in the swamp."

All the color drained from Ally's face. "The *swamp?*" she repeated with panic and disgust.

The musician tipped back his head and laughed. "Y'all aren't from around these parts, are ya?"

Ally and Jordan shook their heads in perfect synchronization.

"*They're* not," Freddie replied. "But my daddy grew up here."

The sax player was instantly intrigued. "I thought you looked familiar. Who's your daddy?"

Freddie opened her mouth to make up some lie—she definitely didn't want anyone here to know who she *really* was—but before she could utter a word, Ally blurted out, "Dr. Facilier! Do you know him?"

And once again, the entire club fell silent. But certainly not for the same reason as before.

The musician's face went from friendly to suspicious in a frightening heartbeat. "What did you say?"

"Nothing!" Ally chirped, covering her mouth. She must have realized her mistake because now every single person in there was glaring at them.

"You say you're related to the shadow man?" the musician asked, sounding more angry by the second.

"No," Jordan was quick to say. "You must have misunderstood."

"There ain't no misunderstanding the shadow man," the musician said sternly. "He put a curse on my grandmother, a real bad one. She never recovered. And I always swore if I saw the shadow man or any of his family again, I would get my revenge."

Freddie could see rage building in the man's eyes.

"Oh, crumbs," Ally said, her voice shaking. "This isn't good."

"Don't panic," Freddie whispered to the girls. "Let's just calmly stand up and leave."

The three of them rose slowly from their seats and started backing toward the door.

"Not so fast," the large musician drawled, stomping ominously after them. The floor seemed to vibrate with each heavy step he took. "I think you and I have some business to take care of."

"Actually," Freddie said, her voice squeaking, "as much as we'd love to stay and chat, we really should be going."

But when they reached the front door, they found another burly musician blocking it, his muscular arms crossed over his chest.

The sax player took another menacing step toward them. "I've been waiting a long time for the shadow man to return."

"What about now?" Ally asked. "Can we panic now?"

Freddie glanced around the small restaurant. There seemed to be no way out. And the scary sax player was getting closer.

They were most definitely trapped.

"Yeah," Freddie said, her stomach clenching. "I think we can panic now."

SHUFFLE!

This is bad. Very bad. (And not in the fun way.)

If there's anything I learned from the isle, it's to shuffle in a scuffle.

Freddie shut her eyes tight. Whatever happened next, she didn't want to see it. Then she heard a loud crash and the sound of something breaking.

Ally screamed.

Freddie opened her eyes to see broken glass scattered on the floor. She froze, panicked, but then she heard Jordan call out, "C'mon, you guys! Through here!"

Freddie turned to see Jordan had climbed out the broken window and was reaching her hands back through.

She helped Ally out first and then reached back in to grab Freddie.

Once the girls were outside the club, they started to run.

Freddie could've sworn she heard someone chasing them, but she didn't dare look behind her to check. She just kept her head down and ran as fast she could, slowing only long enough to make sure Ally and Jordan were still with her.

Scenery started to change around them. Buildings turned to trees, sidewalks came to an end, and soon the paved street they were running on morphed into a muddy dirt road, finally coming to a dead end at a giant body of greenish-black water.

They slowed to a stop and struggled to catch their breath.

"I think we lost them," Jordan said, wheezing, with her hands on her knees.

"I'm so sorry!" Ally cried. "I shouldn't have said anything. It's all my fault. It's just that I don't think before I speak and sometimes things just plop out of my mouth and I can't take them back."

"It's okay," Freddie told her. "We're fine now. We made it."

"But where are we?" Ally asked, spinning around and taking in their rugged surroundings. She eyed the sludgy water in front of them with great skepticism.

Freddie laughed. "I think we made it to the swamp."

Ally leaned forward to peer into the water and shuddered. "Ugh. It looks dreadful. I can't even see the bottom. How are we supposed to get across it?"

"If memory serves," Freddie said, dipping a foot into the water and letting it sink down. The swamp came up to her knee. "It's not very deep. We can walk."

Ally crossed her arms over her chest. "No way. I am *not* walking in that."

"I don't think we have much of a choice," Freddie pointed out. "That musician told us Mama Odie lives *in* the swamp. This is the swamp."

Jordan sighed, hiked up her blue harem pants, and waded into the thick water after Freddie. "What I wouldn't give for a flying carpet right now," she grumbled. "C'mon, Ally."

"You don't understand," Ally replied, pointing at her shiny black shoes. "These are patent leather. They're not swamp-proof."

"That's fine," Freddie said, walking farther into the water. "You stay there. Jordan and I will get *our* problems sorted out and you can just, I don't know, deal with the tea shop yourself."

Freddie knew that would do the trick.

Ally harrumphed, bent down to remove her shoes, and hesitantly lowered her stockinged foot into the water. "This better not get in my hair, though. I just washed it this morning. Eek!" she screamed. "What was that? I just stepped on something slimy! Do you think it was a snake?"

Jordan rolled her eyes. "Don't be ridiculous. Snakes don't live under water."

Ally looked relieved as she stepped in with her other foot.

"Actually," Freddie began, "there *are* a few varieties of snakes that live—" But she was cut off by a single sharp glance from Jordan.

Freddie took the lead and waded into the swamp. She had no idea if she was walking in the right direction, but she wasn't about to let those two know that.

Jordan followed after Freddie, and Ally brought up the rear. She was significantly slower than the other two.

"C'mon, Wonderland!" Jordan called over her shoulder. "Pick up the pace! If Princess Tiana can do it, so you can you!"

"Princess Tiana was a frog!" Ally called back. "If I was a frog, this would be easier."

"That can be arranged," Freddie murmured under her breath.

"Oh, dear! What was that?" Ally cried out, stopping in the water. She blew out a breath. "Never mind. Just a pebble! Keep going!"

Freddie rolled her eyes and trudged on. This was going to take a while.

UP THE ANTE

If Ally thinks she sees one more swamp critter, I'll show her a real swamp critter.

"I do hope I don't catch any strange swamp diseases," Ally said as they trudged farther into the swamp.

"There's no such thing as a swamp disease," Freddie called back to her.

"Oh, sure there is," Ally retorted. "There's swamp flu and sludge fever and mud pox."

"Those aren't real diseases," Freddie grumbled.

Ally continued to argue but Freddie stopped listening. Instead she kept her eyes peeled for signs of Mama Odie's houseboat and suspicious-looking rocks in the water. She'd learned from her father's stories about the bayou that alligators roamed this swamp. They would swim just under the surface, only their eyes poking out of the water. The eyes would usually look like floating pebbles.

As Freddie waded through the murky water, listening to Ally list off more imaginary illnesses, she made a mental note of all of the creatures of the swamp her father had told her about over the years.

Obviously there were the gators. Those were dangerous. The egrets—tall white birds with pointy beaks—were only a problem if you were a frog. Crayfish could pinch you under the water, but nothing deadly. And she wasn't even going to think about the scorpions and anacondas.

But as she ticked off the animals on her fingers, she had the feeling she was forgetting something. Something important. Something big. Something . . .

Freddie heard a vicious snarl and froze in her tracks.

Something like that.

Jordan, who clearly failed to notice that Freddie had stopped, ran right into Freddie's back, nearly knocking her down in the knee-deep water.

"What's the deal?" Jordan griped. "Why are we stop—" But she never finished her question, because suddenly *she* saw the thing too.

It was standing on a rock in the middle of the swamp, like a king of a small island, completely blocking their passage.

It was huge. It was terrifying.

And it was *angry.*

The beast opened its mouth and let out a roar, showing off its humongous fangs.

"What is it?" Jordan whispered, her voice trembling.

"I think it's a—" Freddie started to say, but she was interrupted by Ally, who was excitedly moving *toward* the terrifying creature.

"Aww! It's a big kitty!"

Freddie tried to grab Ally to pull her back, but Ally was already too far ahead and approaching the giant cat, which snarled and hissed at her.

"Come here, pretty kitty!" Ally cooed.

"Ally!" Freddie whispered frantically. "Come back! That's *not* a kitty. It's a cougar!"

But Ally ignored her and kept moving forward, her hand outstretched.

Freddie couldn't watch. Ally was about to get her hand chomped off by a vicious cougar!

The cat roared again and lashed out at Ally with an angry swipe of its paw. Ally yelped and jumped back, landing on her bottom in the swamp water. After a moment, she pushed herself back to her feet and placed her hands on her hips. "How rude!" she scolded the cat. "Naughty kitty! Naughty, naughty kitty!"

The cougar hissed in response, shaking its head.

"Ally," Jordan warned, "I think we need to turn back. That is *not* a kitty. That is a very angry cougar and—"

"No," Ally retorted. "We came this far. I'm drenched in muddy swamp water. I'm covered in mosquito bites. I am *not* turning back just because this kitty doesn't remember its manners."

"Ally," Freddie said, her wide eyes pinned on the cat, "it's a wild animal. It doesn't know any manners."

"Nonsense," Ally insisted. "That's no excuse. Mum says everyone should have good manners. I'll just have to explain that to him."

Freddie was starting to lose her patience. She would've liked to just grab Ally and *drag* her away, but she didn't want to get any closer to that ferocious cat. "Ally, you can't *explain* anything to a wild cougar."

But Ally ignored her. She placed her hands on her hips and in a stern yet patient voice said to the cougar, "Now, you listen here, kitty. Just because you live in a swamp, that does not give you an excuse to be rude."

The cougar hissed and spat, clawing at the air with its mighty paw.

"That's a good point," Ally said, as though actually responding to something the cat was saying. "We *are* strangers walking through your home. So why don't we all get to know each other. My name is Ally. And this is Freddie and Jordan."

Jordan gave a weak, petrified wave, but Freddie refused to move.

"Freddie," Ally admonished. "Say hi to the kitty so you're not strangers anymore."

This is ridiculous! Freddie thought.

Freddie had always suspected Ally was a little peculiar, but now she was sure of it. In fact, this girl had to be mad as a hatter. And she was about to get them all eaten because of it.

"Freddie," Ally warned again.

"Hi, kitty," Freddie said reluctantly.

"Very good. Now what is your name?" Ally asked the cougar.

The cat roared and crouched low, looking like he was ready to pounce.

"Ally," Freddie said. She was terrified now. "He's about to attack."

"Biscuit!" Ally exclaimed. "Well, that's a lovely name."

Biscuit? Freddie thought. *Is she serious? Where does she get this stuff?*

"Now, Biscuit," Ally went on. "I would like you to be a good little kitty and lie down so I can pet your belly."

The cat couched lower, narrowing its dark vicious eyes at Ally and flicking its tail. It was definitely going to attack.

Freddie readied herself to run. Ally could do what she wanted, but Freddie was *not* going to get mauled by a swamp cougar.

"All the way down," Ally commanded, pointing toward the ground with her finger.

Then, just when Freddie swore it was about to spring into the air and make a delicious lunch out of Ally, the cougar lay down instead. Freddie's eyes nearly popped out of their sockets.

Was that a coincidence?

"Good kitty," Ally commended. "Now roll over."

The cat rolled onto its back, his legs sticking straight into the air.

Freddie couldn't believe what she was seeing!

"There you go," Ally said, approaching the cougar. She slowly extended a hand and scratched its stomach. The cat began to purr.

"Is this for real?" Jordan murmured to Freddie out of the side of her mouth, keeping her gaze locked on the scene in front of them.

"I'm not sure," Freddie admitted.

"Good Biscuit," Ally trilled, reaching up to scratch the cat's neck.

The cat purred louder and let his head hang back.

"Pretty kitty."

The cat licked its paw and rubbed its ear, grooming itself. Ally laughed. "Yes, you *are* a pretty kitty. Yes, you are!"

Careful not to scare the creature, Freddie slowly approached and gaped at Ally in wonder.

"What?" Ally asked, seeing Freddie's astonished expression.

"So you really *can* talk to cats?"

Ally tilted her head like she didn't understand the question. "You can talk to anyone."

"No, I mean, they can actually understand what you're saying," Freddie clarified.

Ally stood up and wiped her slightly dirty hands on her dress. "Of course they can, silly."

Then she walked around the rock, where the subdued cougar was still lying, and continued wading through the swamp. Freddie just stood there, still in shock, as she glanced back and forth between Ally and the wild cat, which right then looked no scarier than a stuffed animal.

Maybe she's kind of a genius.

"Hey, slowpokes!" Ally called back to them. "Are you guys coming or not?

Freddie looked at Jordan, who looked back at Freddie.

"Uh, did Ally just save us from a swamp cat?" Jordan asked.

Freddie nodded, still completely stunned by the recent turn of events. "I think she did."

Then, less than thirty seconds later, Freddie heard Ally scream.

SLEIGHT OF HAND

So Ally had a few tricks of
her own up her sleeve.

But now what? We don't have time to be hanging around.

Freddie and Jordan ran as fast as they could through the
sludgy water, which, admittedly, was not very fast. They
reached a thicket of weeds, which were taller than their
heads, and fought to cut through them as they followed
the sound of Ally's screams.

When they finally came to a clearing, Freddie had
to blink to make sense of what she was seeing. Ally was
suspended ten feet in the air, trapped inside a small cage
made out of what looked like bamboo shoots.

Freddie and Jordan each took a step toward her.

"No!" Ally cried. "Go back! It's a—"

But it was too late. Freddie heard a loud *snap*! Suddenly, she felt the ground being ripped out from under her as another giant bamboo cage closed around both her and Jordan and lifted them into the air.

Now all three of them were dangling over the swamp. Ally in her cage hanging from one tree, and Jordan and Freddie in their cage hanging from another.

The cage was *not* roomy by any stretch of the imagination. In fact, it was really cramped. Jordan and Freddie were completely tangled up, to the point where Freddie couldn't tell whose limb was whose.

Jordan started screaming. Ally continued screaming. And finally, feeling left out, Freddie screamed, too.

What had she gotten them into?

Why on earth had she decided to lead two AKs into a swamp? What had she been thinking?

"Okay!" Freddie yelled over the screaming. "Enough! Everyone be quiet so I can think."

"What could you possibly have to think about?" Jordan asked.

"How to get us out of here, obviously!" Freddie snapped.

"What are these things?" Ally asked.

"I think they're frog traps," Freddie replied. "This area is probably filled with frog hunters."

"But we're not frogs!" Ally whined.

"I know that!" Freddie said. "But the traps don't know the difference."

"I mean, seriously," Jordan griped. "I'm used to being stuffed inside a lamp, but *this* is tight." She attempted to stretch out her legs but just ended up kicking Freddie in the face.

"Quit kicking me!" Freddie barked.

"Sorry," Jordan mumbled.

"What are we going to do now?" Ally asked.

Freddie reached her hand through one of the bamboo bars of the cage, feeling around for a clasp or door. She finally located it and was relieved to discover it was a typical lock. Easy to pick.

Except for one problem.

She had nothing to pick the lock *with*.

"Jordan!" she said with sudden inspiration. "Give me your hair pin."

Jordan snorted. "I don't have a hair pin. What makes you think I have a hair pin? It's not the nineteen fifties. Who wears hair pins?"

"I have a hair pin!" Ally called out from the other trap.

"That doesn't do me much good," Freddie said. "You're all the way over there."

"But the traps swing," Ally pointed out.

Freddie was about to argue, but then she realized Ally was right. The traps *did* swing. And if they could just get close enough . . .

"Okay," Freddie said decisively. "Ally, take the pin out of your hair."

"Done!" Ally said after a few seconds.

"Good," Freddie commended. "Now, Jordan. Can you stick your legs out of the cage and reach that tree over there?"

Freddie felt Jordan moving around and then she was shoved against the side of the cage as Jordan fought to stick her legs through the bars. "I can reach!" Jordan announced.

"Great," Freddie said, although the word was muffled because her face was flattened against the bamboo. *"Noh ush,"* Freddie garbled.

"What?" Jordan asked.

"What?" Ally echoed.

Freddie struggled to pull her face away from the side of the cage so she could talk. "I said, now *push*."

"Oh. Duh." Jordan kicked her legs out against the tree and the cage started to swing.

"Ally!" Freddie called. "I need you to catch us."

"Um, okay," Ally said uneasily. "I'll try. I've never been very athletic, though. Mum tried to teach me to play croquet once and I couldn't even—"

"Ally!" Jordan and Freddie both shouted as they sailed right past her.

"Right! Sorry! Give it another go!"

Freddie and Jordan's cage swung back toward the tree and Jordan gave them another hard push.

"Get ready, Ally!" Freddie called.

"I'm ready!" Ally shouted.

The cage soared through the air again. Freddie held her breath and then felt a hard yank as they were pulled to a sudden stop. She released the breath and strained her neck to try to see behind her.

Ally had caught them!

"Gotcha!" Ally said proudly.

Jordan let out a whoop.

"Yes!" Freddie said. "Now don't let go. Hand me the hair pin." She fought to wedge her hand up behind her head and out of the cage. She felt something small and metal being placed in her hand and drew her arm back inside.

Then Freddie got to work on the lock. It was difficult to do from her cramped position because she couldn't actually *see* the lock, but Freddie was a pro. After only a few tries, she heard the soft *click* of the lock disengaging and carefully swung the door open.

Jordan jumped out, landing with a splash in the water below.

With the extra room, Freddie was then able to turn her body around so she could see Ally's cage. She inserted the hair pin into the lock and sprung open the door.

"Whee!" Ally said, leaping down from the cage and making an even bigger splash than Jordan. She no longer seemed to care about the swamp water getting in her hair.

Freddie chuckled and leapt after her.

For a moment, the girls were so happy to have been freed from the frog traps that they completely forgot they were supposed to be mad at one another. They jumped and splashed in the sludgy water, kicking their feet and laughing giddily.

Then Freddie glanced up and her heart sank.

"Um, guys. I'm not sure we should have jumped down from those cages."

"Why?" Ally asked, oblivious to what Freddie had spotted. "Are you afraid of a little swamp juice in your hair?" Ally reached down, scooped up a handful of water, and tossed it at Freddie.

"No," Freddie said, spitting out the water that had splashed into her mouth. "Look." She pointed up at the tree Jordan had used to kick them into motion and suddenly the girls understood.

Nestled high in the branches, like a bird's nest, was a giant boat.

Or *house*boat to be more specific.

Freddie sighed. "I think we found Mama Odie."

BLIND DEAL

We did it! We found Mama Odie!
Now all we have to do is figure out
a way up her crazy front lawn.

And by lawn, I mean tree trunk.

After what felt like hours of difficult climbing, the girls finally reached the houseboat in the tree. There wasn't a proper door, so they just walked right in. The house was almost completely dark inside. It looked like no one had been there in ages.

Freddie started to get a panicky feeling in her stomach.

"Is anyone even here?" Jordan asked.

"It certainly doesn't look that way," Ally replied.

"Are we in the right place?" said Jordan.

Freddie was starting to wonder the same thing when, suddenly, a female voice spoke, startling all three of them.

"What took you so long? I was just about to give up on you three."

The girls whipped their heads in the direction of the sound, and that's when Freddie saw, with the help of a single shaft of light coming through a window, the outline of a rocking chair in the corner.

The chair began to rock gently back and forth, and Freddie could just make out the faint silhouette of a woman sitting in the chair.

"Hello?" Freddie asked, taking a tentative step toward her. "Mama Odie?"

The woman in the rocking chair turned on a small gas lamp on the table next to her and the girls let out a gasp upon seeing her face.

Mama Odie was so . . . so . . .

Young.

Freddie could have sworn her father had always described her as an ancient blind lady with a cane. This woman—no, this *girl*—didn't look much older than Freddie.

She had long honey-colored hair that fanned out around her shoulders and big brown eyes that were lined with gold shadows.

Had Mama Odie spelled herself into a younger woman?

"Are you—" Freddie started to ask, but the girl finished the question for her.

"Mama Odie? Afraid not. I'm her daughter, Opal."

"Oh," Freddie said. That made much more sense. "Do you know—"

"When she'll be home?" Opal finished. "No, I don't. I'm holding down the fort in her place. You know, stirring the gumbo pot. Feeding the snake."

Ally leapt in terror. "SNAKE? Where's a snake?"

"Don't worry. He's perfectly harmless. I think he really likes your hair."

Ally screamed and started running her hands frantically through her hair. "Get it off! Oh, dear! Get it off of me! Now!"

Jordan came over to help, grabbing Ally by the arm. "Hold still. I'll find it." But after combing through Ally's hair, she found nothing. "There's no snake in your hair."

Opal broke out into a bold deep-bellied laugh. "Oh, that was too much fun! So *you're* the gullible one. I just had to check. My visions weren't super clear on which one it would be."

"Gullible one?" Ally repeated, offended. "I am *not* the gullible one."

Jordan and Freddie both gaped at her.

"Okay," Ally admitted. "So maybe I'm a little quick to believe a few things, but that doesn't make me gullible. It makes me *trusting*."

But Freddie wasn't listening to anything Ally was jabbering on about. She was too busy thinking about what Opal had said just before that.

Visions? Freddie thought. *Did she just say visions?*

"Yes," Opal replied, as though responding to the question in Freddie's head.

"Yes, what?" Freddie asked.

"I did say visions."

Freddie's mouth fell open. "You can read my thoughts?"

Opal clucked her tongue and rocked back and forth in the chair. "Well, not *all* of them. The stronger ones, yes. It was harder when you guys were far away, but as you got closer to the boat, they started to become clearer."

Ally narrowed her eyes at Opal. "Are you a VK?"

Opal squinted. "A what?"

"What she means is," Jordan explained, "are you a villain kid?"

Opal threw her head back and laughed that same bold laugh. "You think just because my mom has pet snakes and can cast voodoo spells that she's a villain?"

"Well . . ." Ally hesitated.

But Opal didn't let her finish. "Never mind. I can already read the answer."

"In my mind?" Ally asked, flabbergasted.

"No. On your face."

Ally quickly tempered her expression.

"Anyway," Opal said, "you clearly have a lot to learn about villains."

"Oh, I think we know plenty," Ally mumbled, darting a look at Freddie.

"Ah, yes," Opal said knowingly. "The Shadow Cards. The reason you're here, right?"

"We came to see if your mom could reverse the spell," Freddie clarified. "We're worried the cards might cause more bad things to happen."

"Those shadows are tricksters, aren't they?" Opal rose from her chair and sashayed over to the giant bubbling black pot in the center of the room. She gave it a quick stir, then dipped her finger in and licked it. "Mmm, mmm, mmm! I do make a mean gumbo."

"So," Freddie prompted, starting to lose her patience. "*Can* your mom reverse a spell cast by Shadow Cards?"

"Of course she can," Opal said. "And so can I."

Freddie nearly wilted in relief, and she heard Ally and Freddie let out simultaneous sighs.

"But she won't," Opal said matter-of-factly. "And neither will I."

Freddie instantly deflated. "What?"

"We don't use magic anymore. We're not really supposed to. King Beast's orders. Now this magic gumbo pot is filled with just regular ol' gumbo." She took another taste. "But man, is it some *good* gumbo!"

"B-b-but," Freddie stammered. "But this is an emergency. You have to make an exception."

Opal sighed dramatically. "It always is, isn't it? Everyone who comes here looking for Mama has some kind of *big* emergency."

"But we really do!" Jordan said, stepping forward. "My Web show has been canceled! And Ally's parents' tea shop is flooded and our friend Carlos has a dislocated shoulder and can't play tourney."

Opal turned toward them with wide, concerned eyes. "Really?"

"Yes!" Ally said, stepping up beside Jordan.

"That's horrible!" Opal cried. "Why didn't you say so in the first place?"

"So, you'll help us?" Freddie asked.

Opal laughed. "No. But you should have seen your faces. So full of hope."

Ally let out a grunt. "You *are* a VK!"

"Honey," Opal said condescendingly. "There's a big difference between being a villain and being just plain sassy."

"But," Freddie complained, "I don't understand. If you have the ability to help us, why won't you?"

Opal smiled. It was a genuine smile this time. "Because," Opal said kindly, "you don't *need* my help. Or my mother's."

"Yes, we do," Jordan argued. "We really, really do."

Opal shook her head and went back to stirring the gumbo pot. "Sweetie pies," she said silkily, "you already know how to fix your problems. All of them."

Freddie frowned, confused. "No, we don't. That's why we came here."

"Well, see," Opal said, adding a dash of hot sauce to the pot and stirring again. "That's the thing. Everything you need, you already *learned* on the journey here."

"What?" Freddie asked. "No, we didn't."

Opal turned from her pot and stared intensely at Freddie. "Aww, have faith in yourself, sugar plum," Opal said soothingly. "Besides, I know for certain you'll figure it out."

Freddie squinted "How do you know?

Opal gave her a coy wink. "Because I've already seen it happen."

Freddie felt frustration boiling up inside her.

Why is Opal being so difficult? Why can't she just tell us straight up what to do?

"Now, where would be the fun in that?" Opal said, once again answering the question in Freddie's mind. "If I told you exactly what to do, you'd miss out on the adventure of discovering it yourself."

Freddie shook her head. "I don't *want* any more adventures! I just want to fix this."

"And fix it you will," Opal said confidently as she lowered herself back down into the rocking chair. "As my mama always said, 'you just gotta dig a little deeper.'"

GAME OVER

What a waste of a day. We're no
closer to fixing anything.

Leaving the bayou. #ByeYou

"Well, that was a huge waste of time," Jordan said as soon
as they were out of the houseboat and back in the swamp.

"Yeah," Ally agreed, glaring at Freddie. "What are we
supposed to do now?"

But Freddie couldn't answer that question, because she
didn't know. This was her big plan. She had been so certain that if they went there Mama Odie would help them.
But they didn't even get a chance to see Mama Odie.

What was all that mumbo jumbo about not need-
ing her help? That Freddie already knew how to fix all
of their problems? Of course she didn't already know! If

she already knew, she wouldn't have dragged two whiny Auradon kids through the swamp.

How much deeper could she dig? What could Opal even mean?

With a sigh, Freddie turned and walked away.

"Wait!" She heard Jordan's angry voice behind her. "Where are you going? What's the plan now?"

"There is no plan," Freddie mumbled dejectedly. "We just go home."

But even as she said the words, she wondered what they meant. *Go home.* Where was home for her? Auradon Prep? The Isle of the Lost? The bayou?

None of them really felt like home.

None of them really felt like places she wanted to go back to.

So where would she go from there?

As they trudged through the swamp, Freddie added that to the list of questions she still couldn't answer.

The drive back to Auradon was as awkward as the one to the bayou. No one talked the entire trip. Whatever kind of bond the three of them had managed to build in the few hours they had spent traversing lakes of mud and escaping cougars and frog traps was long gone.

For a moment there, Freddie had actually felt like

she was a part of something. A group. A trio. A team. Those AKs never would have survived that swamp without her.

Actually, when Freddie really thought about it, they had all contributed in some way. If Ally hadn't known how to talk to cats, they never would have gotten past the cougar. And if Jordan hadn't busted a window in the jazz club, they never would have escaped that angry musician.

But apparently all of that was only temporary, because now everyone had gone back to ignoring one another.

As Jordan drove the orange Bobbidi Buggy back to Auradon Prep, Freddie closed her eyes and tried to "dig deep" like Opal had told her. She tried to find the answer that Opal had sworn was already inside her.

She tried and she tried, but all she could feel was that horrible sickening sensation in her stomach. The one she hadn't yet been able to identify. But she felt it whenever she thought about Ally's face when they had walked into the flooded tea shop, or Jordan's face when she'd told Freddie about her suspended Web show. Or when she pictured Carlos getting carried off the field with a busted shoulder.

I wish I had never come to the bayou, Freddie thought.

I wish I had never tried to help anyone.
I wish I had never found those Shadow Cards.

Later, Jordan pulled the minivan up the long, curving driveway of Auradon Prep and parked. The girls got out of the car in silence.

"So," Freddie said awkwardly when they'd reached the dorms. "What are you guys going to do now?"

"I'm going to sit alone in my lamp and *not* film my Web show," Jordan said with a huff before turning on her heels and stomping away.

Ally sighed. "I'm guess I'm going to try to clean up the tea shop as best as I can before Mum comes home tomorrow. But I'll never finish in time."

Freddie fidgeted with the hem of her dress. She knew there was something she was supposed to say in this moment. Something appropriate. Something *nice*. It was bubbling on her lips. It was struggling to get out.

But her villainous tendencies were fighting against her. She had been a VK for so long, she had lived in that world for so many years, it felt almost impossible *not* to be one.

Freddie glanced out of the corner of her eye at her shadow on the ground. It looked small and defeated. And about as uncomfortable as Freddie felt.

"What if I helped?" she blurted out before she could stop herself.

Ally blinked her large blue eyes in confusion. "What?"

Freddie sucked in a breath and forced herself to say the words. "What if I helped you clean up the tea shop?"

Ally seemed to comprehend something and shook her head adamantly. "Oh, no. No more Shadow Cards. No more favors from the all-powerful queen of shadows. I can't afford it. The price is just too high."

"No," Freddie rushed to say, taking a hesitant step toward Ally. Ally took a hesitant step away. "No cards. Just me. I'll help you clean up. With two people, it'll go much faster. Maybe we can even finish before your mom gets home."

Ally narrowed her eyes in suspicion. "What's the catch?"

Freddie shrugged. "No catch. No deal. I promise. I just want to help. I feel . . ." She struggled to find the right word, to identify that yucky feeling in her gut. And then it came to her.

"Guilty," she finished softly. As soon as she said the word, she knew it was the right one. She felt guilty. She'd never experienced that sensation before. It was an awful, evil feeling. And not the fun kind of evil, either. She *hated* it.

"Guilty?" Ally repeated with skepticism.

"Yes," Freddie said. "I feel guilty about what the cards did—" She stopped herself and restarted. "I mean, what *I* did, and I want to help make it right."

Ally studied Freddie for a long time, her mouth twisted to the side, as though she couldn't decide whether or not to believe her. "No magic?" she confirmed.

Freddie drew a cross over her chest. "No magic."

Ally surrendered with a sigh. "Okay. Let's go." She turned and started in the direction of the tea shop. "You're right, it will go faster with two people."

Freddie grinned, feeling the knot in her stomach loosen for the first time, and jogged to catch up, her shadow dragging behind.

"All-powerful queen of shadows?" Freddie repeated as she fell into step with Ally. "I kind of like that."

Ally nodded. "I know, right? It has a nice ring to it."

DAMP SPIRITS

It's no shovel, but this bucket is
digging deep and helping.

Maybe Opal had a point. . . . Time will tell.

After working for hours with buckets, mops, towels, blow-dryers, and fans, Ally and Freddie finally got the tea shop dry. By the end of the night, Freddie's arms ached and she was exhausted, but when she stood back to admire what they'd done, she couldn't help feeling a twinkle of pride.

The Mad for Tea shop looked almost as good as new. Sure, there were still a few damp spots on the rugs and some of the furniture wouldn't dry until the morning, but they had done it. And Freddie had never seen Ally look so happy. The smile on her face was practically its own source of sunlight. She was beaming.

Even Freddie smiled a little, despite herself.

"Thank you," Ally said as Freddie was leaving to head back to the dorm. "It was really nice of you to help me out."

Freddie shrugged. "It was the least I could do."

The whole way back to the dorm, Freddie thought about what had happened that day. How she'd failed to reverse the Shadow Cards' curse, and how she still didn't know what Opal had meant when she'd said that Freddie already knew the answer.

Everything was still a mess. Sure, the tea shop may have been dry, but she still wasn't a member of the Auradonnas. And Carlos was still in the infirmary with a dislocated shoulder. And Fairy Godmother still wouldn't let Jordan film any Web show episodes.

Freddie knew Jordan was upset over it. She had a feeling Jordan felt the same way about her Web show as Freddie felt about singing.

"Wait a minute," Freddie said aloud, as a thought suddenly came to her. She stopped walking. "Fairy Godmother said *Jordan* couldn't film another episode."

Freddie covered her mouth to stifle a gasp. Then she took off at a run.

She found Jordan in the banquet hall a few minutes later, sitting alone at a table with her laptop, hitting refresh over and over.

Jordan momentarily looked up when she heard Freddie enter. "I just lost fifty more followers. In an hour," she lamented.

Freddie ignored her. "I know how to fix it!" she shouted breathlessly.

Jordan scowled. "Fix what?"

"Your Web show."

"There's nothing to *fix*," Jordan said. "I'm not allowed to film any episodes."

"Yes," Freddie said, a huge grin spreading across her face. "*You're* not allowed to film any episodes. But Fairy Godmother didn't say anything about *me*."

WILD CARD

I'll take over Jordan's show
for now! It'll be great.

This is definitely one of my more brilliant
ideas. Why didn't I think of it before?

"And that's a wrap!" Jordan called three hours later. It was dark out and everyone else had gone to bed, but Jordan and Freddie had just finished editing the most epic episode of Jordan's Web show ever.

Well, Freddie thought it was the most epic ever, but to be fair, she hadn't seen that many episodes. She still wasn't exactly sure what Jordan's Web show was about.

"Play it back!" Freddie said excitedly.

The two girls had spent the last few hours film-ing Freddie singing different parts of the same song in various locations all over the school. And now with a little editing magic, they'd turned her into a one-woman a cappella group!

Jordan pressed play and Freddie appeared on the screen, four times. The screen was split into quarters and Freddie's face was in each square. In the top left square, she sang the soprano part of the song; in the top right square, she sang the alto part. In the bottom left, she sang a groovy background harmony. And finally, in the bottom right, she snapped and made short hissing sounds with her teeth to form the percussion part of the track.

Separately, the parts had sounded pretty weird, but edited all together and layered, it sounded perfect.

It was the same song she'd sung in Bass Notes and Beignets, right before they had been chased out of the club—the Auradonnas' finale number, "Would You Rather?"—except now it was a cool jazz remix.

"That sounds totally wicked," Jordan remarked after the song had come to an end. "My viewers are going to love it. Are you ready to post?"

Freddie grinned. "Ready."

With a flourish, Jordan pressed a key on her laptop and both girls gathered in front of the screen to watch the view counter. Freddie held her breath. How long would it take before—

"Look!" Jordan cried. "We got our first viewer."

"And there's another one!" Freddie said as the little number under the video clicked from one to two. After that, the number of views skyrocketed. It went from two to twenty in a matter of seconds. And from twenty to two hundred a few minutes after that.

"Whoa!" Jordan said. "This is good."

"Do you think people are liking it?" Freddie asked.

"Of course they are!" Jordan said. "Look at those comments."

Freddie hadn't even noticed that comments had already started appearing beneath the video. She read the first few.

Best episode yet!

Who is this Freddie person? She has wicked good chops.

We'll miss you, Jordan! But thanks for stepping in, Freddie!

Freddie beamed at the screen, pride bubbling up in her chest. She had finally gotten to sing, and in front of all of those people. And they loved it!

She glanced over at Jordan, who was also beaming. Then she looked at the screen, where the video had started over, and she could hear her own voice reverberating out of the speakers. Ever since she was a little girl, her big dream had been to become a singer. It was the only reason she was in Auradon. And until a few minutes ago, she'd felt like that dream might *never* come true.

After filming the Web show, Freddie decided it was time to visit Carlos in the hospital. She hadn't yet seen him since he'd dislocated his shoulder. Mostly because she'd felt too guilty, but now, she realized he was only there because of her—because *she* trusted the Shadow Cards—and she needed to apologize.

"Apologize?" Carlos said with a wrinkle of his nose. He was lying in one of the infirmary beds with his arm in a sling, slurping a milkshake out of a straw. Dude was curled up in a little fur ball on the foot of his bed.

"I know," Freddie said with a chuckle. "It's not a word that gets tossed around much on the Isle of the Lost."

"I'm not sure it's a word that's even *known* on the Isle of the Lost."

"Yes," Freddie admitted. "But it's a word that's used here. And if this is going to be my home, then I guess I have to learn the language of the natives."

Carlos flashed her a look of disgust. "You're not going to hug me or something, are you?"

"Eww. No!" Freddie said instantly.

Carlos exhaled loudly in relief. "Thank badness."

Freddie grabbed a spare pillow from the empty bed next to him and swatted him with it.

"Hey!" Carlos complained, protecting his milkshake with his good arm. "Watch it! This is chocolate malt!"

"I'm not going to hug you," Freddie continued. "But I do want to help somehow."

"Help?" Carlos once again pronounced the word like he'd never heard of it before.

Freddie nodded toward his busted arm. "Yeah, I feel bad that you're stuck in here and can't play tourney."

Carlos snorted. "So what are you going to do? Strap on body armor and a helmet and storm the tourney field in my place?"

"I'd probably play better than you," Freddie teased.

Carlos grabbed the pillow Freddie had used to swat him and threw it at her. She ducked just in time.

Dude startled at the commotion and jumped off the bed. He ran over to the door of the infirmary room and scratched at it, letting out a soft whine.

"Actually," Carlos said, his voice softening. "I could use your help with Dude."

Freddie's gaze swiveled toward the furry mutt waiting by the door. "Your dog?"

"Yeah. He's getting antsy cooped up in here all day. The doctors said I have to take it easy for a few more days, but he's used to going on walks and running around the tourney field and—"

"I can take him for a few days," Freddie interrupted, feeling the last bit of guilt dissolve in her stomach the moment she said it. "I'm happy to help."

"Happy?" Carlos echoed, once again pretending he didn't know the meaning of the word.

Freddie nodded. "Okay, yeah, I might have overdone it with that one."

FACE UP

I may not be willing to call myself "happy"—
I am a villain's kid after all—but I'm walking
with my head a little higher . . . and this
fluffy little shadow following me around.

For the next hour, Freddie walked Dude around the campus of Auradon Prep. The dog loved it. He stopped to sniff every tree and every flower. She took off his leash and he ran ahead of her, leaping with delight.

As night began to fall and the streetlamps turned on, illuminating the path in front of her, Freddie could feel her shadow fall into step beside her. It was almost like it was tapping her on the shoulder, reminding her that it was there. Always waiting to show itself.

She stopped and turned toward the dark formation on the sidewalk.

Because of the way the light shown dramatically behind her, her shadow was *huge*. It stretched across the path and onto the green grass. It looked so menacing. And the tiny top hat with the peacock feather that Freddie always wore made it look like her shadow had a grotesque, distorted head.

"I'm not afraid of you," Freddie announced.

The shadow didn't move. It didn't run. It didn't hide.

Not that Freddie expected it to.

She extended her arm out to the side and watched her dark silhouette do the same.

She took a step to the left. Her shadow followed.

She crouched down low. Her shadow morphed into a tiny black blob on the sidewalk.

Freddie glanced up at the street lamp above her head. She was standing right in the middle of its soft beam. She took three giant steps to the left, until she was completely out of the light.

Her shadow disappeared.

Freddie let out a maniacal laugh as something dawned on her that she'd never realized before.

All this time, she'd thought her shadow followed her. Stalked her. Wreaked havoc on her life and the lives of people around her. But actually, it wasn't like that at all.

Her shadow was a prisoner. It was trapped. It could

only go where she went. It could only do what she did.

Her father may have been controlled by dark creatures and shadowy figures, but Freddie wasn't.

With another laugh, she jumped back into the light, watching her faithful shadow appear again.

Except it wasn't alone. A second silhouette appeared next to it. This one was wide and lumpy.

Freddie jumped in surprise and turned around to find Evie carrying a giant sack over her shoulder.

"Whatcha doin'?" Evie asked in an amused tone.

Embarrassed at having been caught standing in the dark, laughing with her own shadow, Freddie tried to act natural. "Nothing. Just out for a walk with Dude."

Upon hearing his name, Dude came running over from a bush he'd been sniffing.

It was clear, though, that Evie didn't believe Freddie for a second. But thankfully she didn't press the issue. Instead, she swung the giant sack from her shoulder and let it drop to the ground. "Ugh, this thing is heavy."

"What is that?" Freddie asked.

Evie opened the bag to reveal layers upon layers of shimmery fabrics. "They *were* the costumes for Ben's tour. The sewing club and I made the most amazing capes for his entourage. But then the tour was delayed and now I don't know what to do with them."

Freddie pulled one out and examined it. "These are amazing!" she said, running her fingers over the gold fabric and gold stitching.

Evie beamed. "Thanks!"

Freddie pulled out another cape. This one was purple. "They're so . . . so . . ."

"Useless?" Evie finished with a sad chuckle.

"No!" Freddie said with sudden inspiration. "I was going to say flashy."

"Yeah. I know. We were really proud of them. Too bad no one will wear them. At least not until the tour is back on." Evie took the capes from Freddie and returned them to the bag. She cinched it up and heaved it back onto her shoulder. Then she started to walk away.

"Wait," Freddie said with sudden inspiration.

Evie stopped and turned back. "What?"

"If you're not going to use them," Freddie said, "I actually know someone who's in need of some really flashy costumes."

BAD AURA

It's finally the day of the big a cappella
championships. Everyone at Auradon
Prep has been talking about the
Auradonnas and whether or not they
can beat the Sword in the Tone.

If anyone needs me, I'll be moping in my room.

Even though the competition was being held right there
on campus, Freddie couldn't bring herself to go. It was
just too hard to watch them perform up there without
her. Especially when she knew she deserved to be up
there, too. She *should* be up there. And maybe she would
have, if she hadn't messed up her chances by using those
stupid Shadow Cards.

"What do you mean, you aren't going?" Evie asked when she stopped by Freddie's dorm room the morning of the competition. "Everyone is going."

"Not me," Freddie grumbled. She was lying on her bed with Dude, who seemed to be brooding right along with her.

"The capes look fantastic, by the way. Ally was so happy when I gave them to her. That was a really good idea."

Freddie could tell Evie was trying to make her feel better, but it wasn't working. She reached out and scratched Dude behind the ears. He lifted his head and gave her a sad look.

Evie sat down on Freddie's bed. "Sulking causes wrinkles, you know."

"I don't care," Freddie said, but it was muffled and barely understandable because she said it into the pillow.

"You should come," Evie said. "We can sit together."

Freddie shook her head. "I just want to be alone."

Dude barked.

"Sorry. *We* just want to be alone," Freddie corrected herself.

Evie sighed and stood up. "Okay. Well, I'll be in the chapel if you change your mind."

"I won't," Freddie called after her, and then she heard the door close.

She lay on her bed, listening to the footsteps of people in the hallway. Everyone was leaving to go to the chapel. Everyone was leaving to watch the Auradonnas perform without her.

Finally, after what felt like hours, the entire dorm fell silent. Freddie guessed she and Dude were the only ones left in the building.

She pushed herself up and stared at the lonely pink ruffled bed across the room. She really wished she hadn't destroyed all of CJ's pirate decorations in her moody outburst the other night. She missed looking at them. They reminded Freddie of her friend. Now she had nothing but pink ruffles to look at, which just reminded Freddie of everything she wasn't. And everything she'd lost in the past few days.

She reached under her pillow, where she'd stashed the deck of Shadow Cards, and untied the string, giving the cards a quick shuffle. She could feel them coming to life again in her hands. Like her touch alone was enough to activate the dark magic within.

Even Dude seemed to feel it, because he suddenly picked up his head and growled at the cards.

The all-powerful queen of shadows.

That was who she had become. That's what the cards made her.

But as she held the powerful objects in her hands and stared down at the creepy images drawn on the faces of each one, Freddie began to realize that she didn't want that title. She didn't want to be known for her dark magic. She wanted to be known for what was truly important to her: singing.

And the cards had only made a mess of things.

She carried the deck over to the fireplace, dropped the cards inside, and pulled the pack of matches from her pocket. She ran her fingers over the writing on the back.

BASS NOTES AND BEIGNETS

After what had happened, she wasn't sure she'd ever be able to set foot in there again.

She lit a match and tossed it into the fireplace. The cards instantly caught fire, blazing up in a bright purple glow that seemed to flicker and squirm, like it was trying to hold on. Trying to stay alive. But it couldn't. The purple light that once belonged to those magic cards fizzled and popped and then slowly faded away. Freddie swore she could hear the tiny screams of shadows being snuffed out. Of dark magic being destroyed.

Just as the very last card shriveled and turned to ash, there was a knock at the door. A moment later, Evie burst into Freddie's room again.

"Freddie! You have to come to the chapel quick!"

Freddie groaned. "Evie, I told you, I'm *not* going to the compet—"

"You have to!" Evie interrupted. "Something happened to Ally!"

That got Freddie's attention.

"She lost her voice!" Evie explained breathlessly.

"What? How?"

Evie shook her head. "I don't know. She said she contracted something from swallowing swamp water. Something called slime disease?"

Freddie rolled her eyes. "That's not a real thing!"

"It doesn't matter! Her voice is gone. The Auradonnas made it into the final round, but she can't sing. If they don't have twelve members, they'll be disqualified. You're the only other person who knows the competition song. You have to step in for her."

Freddie curiously glanced back at the fireplace and

what was left of her Shadow Cards. They were now just glowing purple embers.

Did something happen when I destroyed those cards? Or is this just a coincidence?

Either way, Freddie wasn't about to waste time thinking about it. She had an a cappella championship to get to.

LUCKY DRAW

Good thing I practiced singing all those songs!
It's time for me to take my place on stage.

I can't believe this is actually happening
after everything that went down.

"What is *she* doing here?" Audrey asked when Freddie and Evie burst into the Auradonnas' dressing room.

"I'm here to sing Ally's part," Freddie said. "I know it. I can do it."

"No way," Audrey said, crossing her arms. "I'm not allowing a VK to join the Auradonnas."

"But Audrey," Jane argued timidly. "Without her, we'll be disqualified and the Sword in the Tone will win by default! She's the only person who knows all of our songs."

"That's right," Freddie said with a smug smile. "I'm all you got. So you either sing with me or you don't sing at all."

Audrey looked visibly torn. Every girl in the group was staring at her, and Freddie could've sworn she saw a vein pop out in Audrey's neck. The girl was clearly *not* happy about this development.

"Fine," Audrey said with a huff, tossing Freddie an extra-shimmery cape. "Whatever. You just better not mess up or—"

"Oh, I won't," Freddie said confidently, catching the cape with one hand.

Then an announcer's voice came over the speaker. "Welcome to the final round of our a cappella championship, where the Sword in the Tone will battle it out against the Auradonnas for the title of national champions! Up first, with their final performance, let's welcome to the stage the Sword in the Tone!"

Nervously, the girls all left the dressing room and scurried to the wings of the stage, where they could watch their competition in action. Their leader—a tall, princely looking guy—called out the count. "Five, six, seven, eight."

As soon as the group started singing, a tangible panic rose among the Auradonnas.

"Good, bad, dark, light. What you rather be tonight?"

"B-b-but, they can't do that!" Jane stammered in a whisper.

Freddie glanced around the group, noticing the horrified expressions on the faces of her fellow singers.

The Sword in the Tone were singing *their* competition song.

It was *their* finale song.

Audrey called everyone back to the dressing room for an emergency meeting.

"This is horrible!" Jane said, on the verge of tears. "They stole our song!"

"We don't know for sure that they stole it," another girl said calmly. "Maybe it's just a coincidence."

"It doesn't matter," Audrey said. "The point is we're doomed. We don't have any other songs prepared. We might as well just admit defeat and pull out of the competition."

The girls looked to each other and then solemnly nodded their agreement. Jane started to cry.

Freddie felt her stomach clench.

No! she thought. She'd worked too hard and suffered through too much to quit before she even had a chance to get up on that stage. But she couldn't deny the fact that Audrey was right. There was no point in going out there and doing the exact same song the exact same way; it would only make them look like fools. And it was impossible for them to learn a brand-new competition song in the next five minutes.

Unless . . .

"Wait a minute," Freddie blurted out, causing everyone in the group to look at her. "Maybe we don't have to drop out."

Audrey narrowed her eyes at Freddie. "We can't get up there and sing the same song."

"I agree," Freddie said. "But we can get up there and sing a *different* song."

"Were you not even listening to anything I said?" Audrey spat. "I just told you, we don't have any other songs prepared. And we don't have time to learn a new one."

"That's the thing," Freddie said with a sly smile. "We don't necessarily have to learn a *new* song to be able to sing a *different* song."

Now everyone just looked confused, which made Freddie laugh and Audrey scowl.

"Gather around, everyone," Freddie said, taking control of the situation. "I have an idea. Did everyone see Jordan's Web show this week?"

"Follow my lead," Freddie assured the group as they walked out of the dressing room a little while later. "It's going to be great."

The moment they took the stage, Freddie could feel butterflies flapping in her stomach. She couldn't believe that after everything she'd done to get there she was still nervous!

Calm down, she silently told herself. *You were born to be up here.*

The lights were off and the Auradonnas all silently took their places.

Freddie grinned in the darkness, excited about what they were going to do. It was risky, but Freddie was certain it would pay off. They were going to knock the judges' socks off with this.

Everyone was in position. The lights came on, and Freddie counted off. "Five, six, seven, eight."

Jane and the other altos kicked off the percussion, then Audrey and the sopranos came in with some background accompaniment. Freddie glanced at the audience, waiting for its reaction. She spotted Evie and Mal in the third row and saw Evie's face fill with panic.

Freddie knew what she was reacting to. So far, it sounded like the exact same song the Sword in the Tone had performed just a few minutes earlier.

But not for long.

Freddie counted silently in her head, waiting for her moment.

"Stop!" she called, extending her hand out.

The singers fell quiet. The audience fell quiet. Everyone was waiting to see what would happen next.

Freddie stared into the audience, an intense look in her eyes. She was trying to build up as much suspense as she could. Then, just when people started to squirm, she yelled, "Let's mix this thing up bayou style!"

Jane and the altos started again from the top, this time hitting the percussion beats at half the tempo, just like Freddie had shown them backstage.

When Audrey led the sopranos in with the accompaniment, it wasn't the same upbeat, bouncy sound that it had been just a second ago. Now it was slow. Smooth. Jazzy.

Just like they do down in the bayou.

Freddie launched into her solo and the crowd went wild. She closed her eyes and pretended she was onstage at Bass Notes and Beignets. That the lights were low and the room was dark and she was the star of the club.

"Doesn't matter what we do, cause I'd rather be with you. Rather be with you. Rather be with you . . ."

She crooned that solo like no one in the audience

had ever heard before: With flavor. With power. With rhythm. With soul.

It was the exact same song, but it sounded completely different. It sounded new and fresh and so totally groovy that the rest of the Auradonnas soon couldn't help getting into it. They swayed and danced as Freddie reached the climax of the solo, hitting that high note with all the power of a VK in an AK world.

When she finished, everyone in the audience was on their feet, clapping and shouting and stomping. Freddie's gaze flew to Mal and Evie in the third row. They were both beaming back at her. Evie gave her a thumbs-up.

Even the judges couldn't stay seated. They were up and whistling.

Freddie stood speechless in the middle of the stage, unable to believe what she was seeing.

They loved it.

They really did!

Freddie felt her lips curving into a broad smile.

There was no denying it: this felt amazing. It felt right.

It felt like magic.

"You saved us!" Jane shouted to Freddie over the roar of the crowd. "Take a bow! You deserve it!"

Freddie looked back and forth down the line of

singers who were all smiling from their success. "Let's take one together," Freddie suggested.

The girls joined hands, raised their arms, and bowed.

Freddie felt like she was in a dream. This was all that she'd ever wanted. To perform up there in front of all those people. To prove to everyone in Auradon that she was more than just a villain kid. That she was Freddie Facilier, the *singer*.

And by the looks of it, she had done just that.

LUCKY CARDS

See, I told you villain plans always work out.

Okay, fine, I had a little help from some . . .
Auradon friends. Yes, you heard me right.

An hour later, the Auradonnas were all gathered in the banquet hall with their newly won national championship trophy. Everyone wanted to take a selfie with it.

Freddie stood back, watching the girls snap photo after photo. She just couldn't stop smiling. She'd been in a trance ever since they'd walked off that stage. The beautiful sound of the audience cheering was still echoing in her head and she hoped it never stopped.

"You did it!" someone cried, startling Freddie out of her thoughts. "You're a star!"

Freddie looked over to see Ally standing next to her.

It took Freddie a moment to realize that Ally was *talking*. In a perfectly normal voice.

"Your voice," Freddie said, frowning. "Is it back?"

Ally flashed a cunning smile and whispered, "I never really lost it."

Freddie blinked. "What?"

"You deserved your shot. You deserved to be up there."

Freddie couldn't believe what she was hearing. "You gave up your chance to compete in the finals for me?"

Ally shrugged. "After you helped me with the tea shop and helped Jordan with her Web show, and got us the new costumes, I knew I had to help you out, too."

"So you *didn't* have slime disease," Freddie pointed out smugly.

"Well, no, not really," Ally said. "But I could have! It's a real thing, you know?"

Freddie opened her mouth to argue, but before she could get a word out, Ally turned to the rest of the group and said, "Auradonnas! Listen up!"

The girls stopped taking photos and turned to look at their captain.

"All in favor of Freddie joining our group permanently, raise your hand!"

Eleven hands shot into the air. Everyone looked

around to see who hadn't voted, and all eyes landed on Audrey. She shrank back slightly from the group, her hands clasped tightly in front of her.

Freddie almost had to laugh. After everything she'd done, she *still* hadn't convinced Audrey to give her a shot.

But then, a second later, a miracle happened. Audrey let out a sigh and mumbled "Whatever," before her hand lifted tentatively in the air.

The whole group cheered. Freddie looked at Ally in disbelief. "You got me into the group."

Ally grinned. "That's what friends do."

Freddie squinted. "Friends?"

Ally laughed. "Yes, silly. Friends!"

Freddie was quiet for a moment, before blurting out, "Opal!"

Ally frowned in confusion. "What?"

"That's what she was trying to tell me! That's what she meant when she said I already knew how to fix everything. In the end, we all got exactly what we wanted. But not because of *magic*. Because of *friendship*."

Ally patted her on the shoulder. "Exactly. We're friends now."

Freddie considered that. "But I'll always be from the isle."

"So how about we say you're an honorary AK?" Ally offered.

"Deal." Freddie stuck out her hand and Ally immediately shook it. "But you better not tell anyone I agreed to that."

Ally giggled. "Don't worry. Your secret's safe with me."